Return
Changeling

Ian P Buckingham

GREEN CAT BOOKS

FIRST EDITION
Published in 2021
by GREEN CAT BOOKS
19 St Christopher's Way
Pride Park
Derby
DE248JY
www.green-cat.shop

Return of the Changeling

In loving memory of William Idris Morris Jenkins

Contents

Acknowledgements

The completion of the first three books in The Changeling Saga wouldn't have been possible without the efficient work of Lisa and her team at Green Cat Books, the support of nearest and dearest like Kate, John, Richard, Mark and a host of others. But most of all, we have to thank the many encouraging messages from the growing readership of boys, girls and families who have enjoyed the adventure, especially during the dark days of our very own pandemic, people like Claire and her son Lewis and the many mothers and fathers who have sent photographs and letters with their own stories.

This one's for you.

Enjoy.

Introduction

In this, the third book in The Changeling Saga, having left the safety of Cornish shores and the bosom of their beloved forest home, the family find themselves surrounded by loyal allies from both realms as well as powerful artefacts that allow them to access considerable power. But will unity and determination and love be enough?

Enough to end the poisonous pandemic still spreading to the corners of the earth?

Enough to combat the forces of alienation and evil that slither through the dark days and haunt their dreams
in the middle of the night?

The American continent is still wild and untamed in parts. Could this be the land that finally brings them face to face with a nemesis who knows each of them so well, because she's a part of them?

Worse still, will this latest journey be their last?

Book 1:
Leaving the Rain in Africa

The dark figure slowly raised its skeletal hands into the air, palms upward, chanting.

At first, they felt a breeze building to a gust and then, like a biblical swarm of killer bees, a sandstorm erupted into the grotto. It eddied round the cloaked figure seated on the floor like a rip-current about a headland rock.

Millions of miniscule, stinging jaws of sand then swept over and through the magical barrier, smothering the two men in an abrasive, suffocating blanket of desert in violent exodus.

Within seconds they were overwhelmed, consumed, choking, blinded and fatally disorientated.

The goddess in the hidden cave glowed gold at the gathering of the changeling clan and their pulsating magical relics. The rains had finally come to the thirsty desert and the land had burst into fruitful life in response; a riot of lusciousness, primary-coloured, thirsty petals, soft wings and sweet scent.

On the wall of the goddess's timeless grotto, the painted world map was ablaze with activity, reflecting the healing reach of the enchanted power of the children and their legendary artefacts combined.

With the demise of the source of the evil alien poisonous pandemic that so blighted nature, every continent depicted on the wall now buzzed with a healthy light. This glow marked the impact of the global rainstorm, which was now washing away the sins of several generations, healing the poisoned past. This storm was happening simultaneously on every continent. Every continent bar one.

One of the biggest.

There, to the west, across the greatest ocean, the Americas

glowered stubbornly in darkness. While most of the world slowly healed from the dark magick pandemic, something over the ocean was clearly still very, very wrong.

Elouisa and her father had been in close, if gentle conference, a quiet conversation since his unexpected arrival. He had recovered remarkably well from the bite of the Werewytch's dagger, despite his great age and having been pulled back so dramatically from the cold clutches of death. Now, despite his daughter pleading for him to rest, they had what seemed like a lifetime to catch up on. It seemed his soul badly needed her soothing words and healing touch.

But his urgency hid a less pleasant and troubling purpose. He also had to warn her that, despite her evident relief, danger still stalked them and everything they held dear.

As expected, Holly was on hand as well. She had wrapped her convalescing grandfather in the Rubyrobe, holding back the very many questions for him that were on the tip of her own tongue.

James, Moses and the sangoma witch doctor Houngane, were studying the map for clues, unwittingly throwing animated shapes on the wall as they talked. They had noticed what appeared to be an agitated pod of porpoises repeatedly heading toward the shore in what seemed to be western Canada, while a shadowy flock of dark birds circled overhead.

"That's like the picture we saw in Savannah's cave," mentioned Lucy, casually.

She had wandered in from outside, where she had been watching Henry race a warthog, before he realised it probably thought he wanted it for lunch, felt sorry for it and stopped for a chat instead.

"Yep," she nodded as all faces turned toward her, and her father raised his eyebrows in a silent question. "We were looking at the painting and map of the Legend of the Lost on the wall, on the beach in Porthleven, when my ring…"

But as she said this and inadvertently squeezed the Ravenring, like a reflex, her tale came to life. Black-winged shapes began billowing in waves from her ring, like thick, dark smoke. The iridescent shapes first filled the roof of the grotto. Then, as had happened in Cornwall, started to form a picture on the map.

"See?" said Lucy, calling Savannah over, who was hiding in the shade.

As a sea lover, with a delicate constitution out of the water, she was finding the African desert heat something of a challenge.

As usual, everyone listened when Savannah spoke. Her measured words and delicate voice lapped softly at the listener's inner ear like a gently returning tide.

"Yes, Lucy. It is the very same vision. See how the orca family circles in distress and then…" She looked away as the whales beached themselves violently on the rocks and sand, soon turning the waters crimson in the flickering cave light.

"I can't watch any more, please make it stop."

Despite her sister's obvious discomfort, Lucy knew she had to press on as they needed as much information, as many clues as they could muster. She may be the smallest of the siblings, but she was made of steely stuff.

Alice wandered over at this point, ever one with a nose for a drama. She too was a little tougher than most, a trait that increasingly bonded the sisters despite being raised apart, and soon she was watching with gritty fascination.

While the others viewed the more obvious events unfold in the sea, what Alice saw were the shapes of nature, the patterns that represented land animals, beavers and cougars, elk and squirrels. She also noticed that they were seemingly running from a great fire, a sensation not that unlike the drama that had unfolded back in her beloved Ashridge Forest where she had grown up.

Then her attention was caught by a mighty bald eagle. It flew imperiously above the heads of the fleeing beasts. Then it made its way to the coast where the orcas were still beaching and landed upon what seemed like a great, gnarled tree.

Once there, it folded its wings and froze. With this gesture, the drama ended at once, then all dissolved into drifting shapeless smoke once again.

Lucy, the youngest, was the first to speak. "Well, what does it all mean, Dad?"

James was deep in thought, stroking his chin, and when he looked over, Alice was striking a similar pose, a familial echo that never ceased to stir a smile.

"I don't know for sure, girls, but I have a feeling that, just as we were drawn to this incredible place for a reason, this vision may well herald the fact that we're going to…."

"…be needed over there." Brinn finished his sentence for him from the other side of the cave.

"Sorry, James, I don't mean to interrupt, but Lariza, the seer and Elouisa's gifted sister, has been reporting a version of this same vision for some time now."

"It did not make complete sense until the girls showed up with the necklace and the ring. Now everything else has started falling into place." He paused and took a sip of the healing potion from the leather flask Elouisa offered him, catching his breath as if his ribs pained him.

"The problems we have had with the Firehills has clearly spread like a pandemic around the world, where the great underwater mountains range. The power of the ancient magic items merging forces as of old is countering much of the evil caused."

"You're right," called out Holly, "After all, we never understood what we had lost until we united and really felt how powerful we are together."

This earned reassuring smiles and nods all round.
"But something is still missing," Brinn muttered, while nodding indulgently at Holly's wisdom.

James turned to the statue and pointed at the goddess's belt. "The dagger?" he asked.

At this, almost without thinking, Savannah held out her right hand, palm upward and tentatively presented her own found item. It still bore marks of the battle with the sea wytch, including a dark stain from the bite it took of her.

They all gasped.

"The Jade Athame," hissed Elouisa breathlessly, accepting the item from her daughter's willing hand.

If truth be told, Savannah had not been comfortable with the cold and strangely animated dagger since her discovery in Kynance Cove.

"Where did you find this?" she uttered, breathlessly, sniffing the blade. "It is an incredibly powerful totem of wiccan kind, believed to have been carved from stone by the earth mother herself." Elouisa's eyes glowed with a dark awe as she examined it closely, scraping a nail on the blood stains and carefully depositing the residue in her pocket in a sort of unconscious reflex action.

"It was in a place to which very few could ever venture, cut off from the land. And you may have it with my pleasure, Mother," Savannah said, graciously.

"You see, without the Athame and the other magical items, we would not have been able to activate the portal that brought us here. It's a link, a magical gateway to the ends of the earth."

James was still deep in thought.

"Will this gateway be able to transport people anywhere at all?"

"The legend has it that it will only move those with the blessings. But, of course, the life circle has yet to be properly closed."

"But we are here, and the goddess statue has only the items we now have amongst the family. What else can there be?"

"True, James. But the goddess is the feminine alone and the circle can never be complete without the balance provided by...."

"The masculine," announced the sangoma, who had been listening in silence. "The circle requires the masculine, the presence of the god to sit alongside the goddess, white wolf with

11

black, yin with yang, light with dark, fire with ice to complete the system."

"Quite right," said Brinn. "Quite right, my new friend. So the answer to that part of this eternal puzzle surely awaits in the land yet in darkness, far across that great but troubled sea."

Vancouver Island sits proudly off the west coast of Canada and is renowned for its spectacular scenery, extreme weather, moist air and incredibly bountiful and fecund wildlife on both land and sea.

Much of the large island is covered with ancient rain forests of giant red cedar trees. So it was fitting that the touchstone point for the portal in Canada delivered the magical travellers, with a loud thump, into the giant trunk of an antique tree. It was so big that it accommodated the whole family at once.

The inside of the tree had the dimensions and aura of a cathedral. Shafts of deep red, dappled orange, azure and lemon light seeping in through holes like windows made by its very many fluffy and feathery residents.

From the portal tree, it was only a short trek through the cradling rainforest ferns to the aptly named treehouse where they would be staying, nestled 30 feet in the air.

"WOW!" came the chorus of approving noises from the

children, clearly thrilled by the accommodation arrangements their grandfather had made.

Even Elouisa was impressed by the safe house the druidic network had managed to unearth for the family, especially here, of all places. She had visions of them having to camp out in her Everbag. Not an enviable resort given the contents were so dangerously unpredictable.

"It's not just what you know but clearly who you know too," laughed James, as they made their way up the incredible cedar spiral staircase, past the mystically suspended jacuzzi bath hot tub and into the jaw-dropping open plan living room area, furnished in all-natural (and some magical) materials like wood and stone and star dust.

Carved redwood pillars flanked the main room like palace guards. Everywhere they looked were beautiful works of indigenous art reflecting the spiritual myths and beliefs of the first people to have settled these lands centuries ago. Stylised seals, birds, bears, wolves, salmon, toads and whales brought the room to magnificent life; a riot of art and craft.

"WOW, WOW, WOW!" repeated Holly as her siblings, with the exception of Savannah, simultaneously stripped down to their underwear and ran for the steaming tub, dampened by a slight forest mist on the way.

By the time the first jumped in, however, Savannah was already splashing them with her gloriously translucent tail.

"This place is AMAZING!" Alice laughed, washing the last of the African dust from her fair hair.

"It's like having a bubbly bath in the sky," shrieked Lucy, feeling the heat on her body as well as the light drizzle on her red cheeks.

While her siblings whooped and hollered, Holly was quietly watching something both mysterious and very exciting unfold in the dense shrubbery beneath them.

She thought she had spotted a dark shape when they first arrived and was pretty sure she was right now, as she could see Henry's nose twitching too.

For 30 feet beneath them, watching from the shade, was a pair of dark eyes. And judging by the distance between those eyes, this was no domesticated cat or dog.

So as her siblings soaked and scrubbed, and her parents busied themselves sorting out the sleeping arrangements, Holly pressed the golden clasp on her cloak and in the twinkle of an eye and a scattering of stars, found herself strained through a rainbow into her faerie form. A microsecond later, she was floating down to the deep part of the fern forest on her beautiful translucent wings.

Holly could smell the black bear before she saw it properly, a musky mix of a primal pong. Then she heard its deep-chested panting and instantly sensed that something was wrong. Despite its size, this was a juvenile black bear at best and it would ordinarily still be with its mother.

"Hello," whispered Holly, in her most soothing bear-friendly tone. "Why so nervous, great one?"

Now, ordinarily, the young bear would have run away in surprise, for bears are quite skittish and shy and not the ogrish monsters people think. They are also deeply distrusting of

15

anything that walks on two legs, even if it is so pretty and flies. But there was something about Holly's respectful demeanour that seemed as natural, to her, as the wind rustling in the maple leaves. So she decided to stay and to confide in the faerie.

"I'm lost. I was looking for berries and the tree killers came, and me and Ma were separated. I was all alone last night, and it was horrid. Then I heard the sound of the water up in the person tree and hoped there would be food nearby. There is always food near woohoomans," she snuffled.

Holly could now see the whole of the bear's head and was delighted to see that she had a white flash on the top of her skull.

"My name is Issy or Fleckle," she said, tracking Holly's gaze. Then she added, "Would you happen to have any fruit please, Miss Flutterwings? Or, even better, perhaps a peanut butter sandwich?"

Tofino town is a spectacular site and an awesome sight.

Groups of old colonial-style wood and rock houses are surrounded by crisp, luscious, verdant forest and icy sea, channelled between a series of islands. Here every breath tastes of cold mist, forest, air and sea. It was the freshest and best of domains the children knew.

The ancient land masses cause the water to gurgle at pace through the natural bay, teeming with sea life while the cry of bald and sea eagles fill the brooding sky.

The Savages, or ancient Trelgathwin family, had a hugely exciting hike through the natural rainforest to reach the main town. It was a sensory explosion for the hyper-sensitive and empathic, spotting and smelling and feeling all manner of incredible critters en route. At one point, Henry stopped and sniffed the air excitedly, and the fleet-sighted among them swore they saw what looked like the cream tail of something feline disappear into the shadowy ferns on the trail ahead.

At the end of their walk, they arrived in the town wide-eyed and eager to soak everything up, and soon settled at a dockside café for drinks and a light lunch on the boardwalk.

"I LOVE it here," said Savannah who, if truth be told, was twitching to dive into the crystal-clear waters. It was taking every fibre of her famous resolve to resist. "This climate is so much kinder to a mermaid's complexion than the dust of the desert."

Henry laughed as she said this, then handed her what turned out to be an incredibly tasty shrimp taco from the mobile restaurant van that one of the locals had described as a legendary eating place.

Soon, the large cups of chowder, seafood delights and bottles of soda pop were keeping them so occupied that, for once, silence descended as they chowed down together. All that could be heard were satisfied groans and the shrieks of the raptors, circling in the air above as prolific as seagulls back in Coverack or Porthleven.

Henry was keeping a wary eye on the patterns the birds were flying while he munched. He noticed that they seemed to be congregating on one of the clearings on the opposite bank,

Wandering closer, nibbling a sliver of avocado from his vegetarian taco as he walked, he noticed a large, dark shape on what appeared to be a rocky beach.

"Terrible thing. Terrible business. Never seen anything like it!" announced a cracked voice behind him.

It was a weather-worn, grey-haired and bearded man in a checked, lumberjack-style red shirt who had clearly noticed his interest. He was pointing with his long-stemmed pipe.

18

On a stone bench, a hundred yards or so away, a dark-haired, dusky man who appeared to have a wooden crutch by his side, was clearly paying more attention to the grizzled senior's conversation than he wanted anyone to realise.

"Orcas. They've been hitting that spot for weeks now. Beaching themselves. Sometimes three or four at a time. We've been dragging some back out to sea, but we don't catch them all, sadly. No-one can understand why they're doing it, but it fair breaks my heart."

He was clearly a kindly man, despite his weathered complexion and wild grey beard, and after a brief conversation with the adults, it emerged that he ran a boat-charter business.

Apparently, it was black bear season, so he offered to take the family out for a special sea-faring safari the next day. Of course, this nearly tipped the already excited girls over the edge, especially when he added, "I had to shoo a momma bear from the porch the other night, as this time of year they're really hungry and seem to be growing braver every passing year."

"Ooooh!" said Lucy.

Of course, Holly already had her own private encounter to relay. But for some reason, she decided to keep her new friend to herself. She didn't quite know why but something inside was telling her that her meeting with the young bear had not been completely by chance. And hard-earned experience had taught her that it was normally best to trust her gut.

As the kind old man, who was called Bill 'The Boat' or Cap'n Bill, wandered off, he gave them a wave and a cheerful, "See y'all

19

in the morning. Boat's called Okwaho by the way, you'll notice her, sure enough."

They all finished up and headed to the nearest chandlery to pick up some warmer clothes, given they had arrived from Africa without really packing.

Savannah, however, could contain herself no longer and after asking Holly to cover for her (giving very specific instructions about the colour and cut of the clothes she wanted), she floated off down the slipway. Making sure nobody was watching her, she glided silently into the waters of the ocean inlet, or sound without so much as a pause.

Not even Savannah, however, spotted the same dark figure on the shore who had been listening to the captain, and who now observed as the changeling took to the water.

Using her cloaking ability, Savanah was able to swim confidently across the bay largely undetected but in full view of the holidaymakers sunning themselves outside the cafés and bars, leaving nothing but a slight ripple you would mistake for an eddy.

She was delighted that the wildlife beneath the water was as vibrant as above. Sockeye salmon with upturned snouts and blushing cheeks gathered in the stronger currents, working on the muscles they would need for their incredible spawning journeys up rivers, waterfalls and rapids. They didn't seem too surprised to see her, which suggested that she may not be the first of her kind they had come across.

As she navigated the fast-flowing sound, rockfish of various kinds, from yelloweye through to tiger, popped their heads out.

Word was clearly spreading of a foreign visitor.

A huge school of lingcod, not usually brave enough to venture so close to the bay, kept her talking for a good ten minutes, asking all sorts of questions about Cornwall. Apparently, they had cousins who had travelled there once, and they were keen to know whether rumours about the legendary grumpy sea bass were true.

A couple of spiny dogfish gave her a shy fin wave, causing her to notice that they, and an army of crabs, starfish and assorted crustaceans were feasting on the remains of a very large carcass.

When she took a closer look, she could see that it was the rotting corpse of what appeared to be an orca cow; not a pleasant sight, very distressing and rather sad, but part of the eternal circle of life.

However, as she examined the carcass of the whale, she noticed what looked like a large growth or deformity near the poor creature's blow hole, which may be a clue to how it met its untimely end.

With this worrying discovery in mind, she swam the last few hundred yards to the rocky beach, her target destination.

As she swam to the beach and then walked from the water in one continuous fluid movement, she disturbed a flock of carrion birds feeding on a very similar body. This, however, judging by its large dorsal fin was a male and quite possibly the partner of the orca she had just left under the water.

The sight of such a mighty apex predator in such a wretched state created a solemn, almost reverential atmosphere, like she imagined a state funeral would be. The morbid birds were now waiting in the trees, watching her with hungry eyes. But she was determined to fulfil the task she came here for and had to take a closer look at the dead sea king.

Sure enough, as suspected, it seemed that he had been driven to his fate by a similar ailment to the one that had befallen his mate. The bumpy growths were obvious even from here and must have caused him a great deal of suffering.

Savannah was deeply saddened by what she had seen, especially as she had seen something not dissimilar relatively recently. Judging by the mutations and the discolouration of the affected area, these magnificent Canadian creatures appeared to be suffering from a similar poisoning agent to the effluent that had been leaking into the waters near Mousehole. But what was most terrifying, wasn't so much the fact that the effluent from the Firehills had extended here, it was the prospect of a mutant surviving the poison. It brought back troubling thoughts of the battle with the wereshark in Mousehole. But if something the size and scale of a killer whale was swimming these waters, driven half-mad with rage by the radioactive lava, who on earth would be able to stop it?

She was still thinking these worrying thoughts as she slipped quietly back into the dark, silent water. Yet this time, as she set off across the deep, dark sound, she felt exposed, very vulnerable and apprehensive indeed.

Moses and Houngane the sangoma were sleeping when the unexpected attack came.

The two African magic users had spent a deal of time at the goddess cave since the family left, studying every last detail and ensuring that they find a way to re-seal such an important site for their people.

The changelings had ported some time ago. But in their eagerness to surf the magical ley lines to the Americas, between them nobody had stopped to consider the serious possibility that the sea wytch may not have been finished off by her daughter and could possibly find a way to escape her confinement in the seer's temple.

Such was their over-confidence, they had simply neglected to seal off the port-way properly, a mistake that would prove fatal, for some.

Luckily, the sangomas had taken the precaution of creating a warlock barrier using ground ancestral dust and okapi bone. This was designed to ward off shape shifters and ensure the Tokoloshe kept its distance.

Although they had reached a form of truce with the demon while they studied the goddess cave and had even grown rather fond of its eccentric ways, they did not truly trust it, especially without its mistress.

Moses was the first to stir, when he noticed a new chill and a sort of musty smell. When he opened his eyes, he saw that the cave was now in darkness. The glow had gone completely. Worse still, a dark and shapeless form sat in the entranceway that they had earlier sealed.

His heart started racing as he tried not to reveal that he was awake, while feeling for his knobkerrie, or tribal club.

"I wouldn't do THAT if I were you," spat a voice as cold as crushed ice and as finite as a terminal breath. "Do not delude yourself into believing that you have any hope, any hope at all."
At this, Houngane awoke and leaped to his feet, eyes as wide as the moon, fear spreading across his face.

He was chanting and chattering an incomprehensible stream of what must have been some sort of spell, for the dust barrier started to smoke with a white heat. Shards of coloured light pierced the gloom, glinting off the jangling beads on his eccentric jewellery.
Yet the sinister figure seated in the doorway with its back turned to them, continued to wait impassively, unstirred.

Then they heard it.

Muffled laughter. Malevolent giggling and a raspy hiss.

Suddenly their magical barrier seemed flimsy and inadequate, the cave no refuge but a prison cell or tomb. In a terrifying heartbeat, their predicament had slipped rapidly from bad to worse.

The dark figure slowly raised its skeletal hands into the air, palms upward, chanting.

At first, they felt a breeze building to a gust and then, like a biblical swarm of killer bees, a sandstorm erupted into the grotto. It eddied round the cloaked figure seated on the floor like a rip-current about a headland rock.

Millions of miniscule, stinging jaws of sand then swept over and through the magical barrier, smothering the two men in an abrasive, suffocating blanket of desert in violent exodus.

Within seconds they were overwhelmed, consumed, choking, blinded and fatally disorientated.

Moses collapsed to his knees, feeling desperately for his sleeping bag. When he found it, he blindly pulled the bag sleeve over his head and tucked the entrance beneath his body. This provided some temporary relief. Yet the maelstrom continued the other side of the bag for what seemed like an infinity, until he started to fear that the tough canvas cover would rip and tear.

Eventually, however, the angry swarm of sand did stop, although it was clear that he was mostly buried by the time it did. When he finally plucked up the courage to withdraw gingerly, crawling in reverse from his life-saving sleeve, it took his clogged and painful eyes, stinging with tears, some moments to adjust to what was now a dark and sand-filled cave.

The first thing he noticed was that the hooded figure had

vanished.

Then he noticed that the Teote goddess statue and amethyst archway were glowing with residual heat. This was clear evidence that the portal had recently been used.

Next, he noticed that the Tokoloshe was no longer in its watery glass cage.

But last he realised that Houngane was almost entirely buried beneath the sand and not moving.

Worse of all, however, upon closer examination, Moses could see that his late friend was now clearly missing part of his feet and cruelly, where most of his toes had been, there was little left but bloodied stumps.

Holly tried to entice her new friend to join the family, but she was still feeling a little bashful and reluctant.

"Mother has been quite insistent that we must not become too friendly with the woohoomans," the bear explained as she chomped her way enthusiastically and noisily through the nuts, berries and cereals Holly had brought for her.

She seemed particularly partial to Honey Nut Cornflakes, which was apt.

"Yes, some of the woohoomans can be very bad and have shooting sticks," she announced. "Sorry, I didn't mean to upset anyone," she added quickly.

Holly just smiled, forgetting that she had not bothered to assume her changeling form for today's conversation.

"Whatever you're comfy with," she said, in an understanding tone. "But we really do need to track down your mum. She sounds great and I'm pretty sure she's going to be worried about you."

Holly could hear her siblings readying themselves for the planned boat trip, so she made her excuses and set off to don her own waterproofs before their hike.

The walk to the dock was even more exciting than the first time they had attempted it.

Henry was quite insistent that they were surrounded by wildlife as they trekked, swearing at one point that something quite large, possibly a cougar, or mountain lion, was within sniffing distance.

But despite the distractions, they were soon boarding Okwaho, Cap'n Bill's blue and white-double-decker boat, cheerfully welcomed aboard by the charming veteran sea dog.

"So how do you like her?" he asked with obvious pride.

"I've got some great news for you guys 'n' girls," he announced enthusiastically, while manoeuvring the boat into the main channel.

"You were asking me about the Native Indian tribes? Well I've asked a few friends, including the sons of Wick-in-in-ish and we're going to stop off at Beaver Bay to pay a visit to the Cowichan people, the Coast Salish down from the Cowichan Valley for a hunt."

"There are no passing Mohawk, sadly, Henry. But I've heard that warriors from the Seshaht and Opetchesaht people have travelled from their usual base on the Somass River and when the moon is full intend to celebrate the Lokwana ritual, a wolf dance, what we call a potlatch. If we manage to time this right it will be something phenomenal for y'all to see."

Henry was cocking his head to the side as the old character spoke. He had a habit of doing this when really interested and his ears were particularly attuned to the sibilantic.

He smiled at Henry as he announced the next bit, still directing the boat expertly into the most advantageous current. They were heading to the islands in Barkley Sound and on to Ucluelet.

"You will love the din made by the blowing of horns, the shaking of rattles, and the beating of sticks on drums. They don't stop until they see wolves." As he said this, he made direct eye contact with Henry in what seemed a knowing way. Or perhaps he was just being paranoid.

"Wow" cried Lucy, breaking their gaze. "Will there be dancing?"

She started doing a strange jig of her own on the foredeck, linking arms with Alice who joined in, tapping on her mouth with her palm in a cliched way that would, frankly, have been a bit embarrassing if not so funny.

"Sure will," he laughed. "Let me think. They do the "Panther dance", "Red-Headed Woodpecker jig", "Wild Swan" and the "Sawbill Duck"."

When he announced the last, he briefly made the shape of a duck bill and did his own mini-jig, flapping his crooked arms as wings, making the girls giggle.

"They are all amazing to watch."

The boat knew this stretch of water so well, but for the visitors it was a wonderland, the air so clean and crisp you could almost taste it and the blue light making the sea dance and sing.

It was all Savannah could do to stay on the deck, so strong was the compulsion to dive overboard and explore the complementary sub-aqua world.

But they certainly weren't bored travelling.

A happy band of seals hogged the tiniest of rock platforms and appeared to wave in their wide-eyed and whiskery, knowing way as they passed.

Soon they were slowing down, as they rounded a bend on the peninsula.

"This is one of the spots where the hungry bears like to come down the shore to search for crabs at this time of year," announced their captain. "Best keep those eyes peeled, kids, for they sure love peelin' crab shell."

They all rushed over to one side of the boat, some with binoculars to scan the long grass that swept down to the long, beach shore.

Henry was instinctively sniffing the air but struggling a little as it was a seaward wind and therefore not bringing any scent from the shore. Oddly, however, he was still picking up quite a strong mammalian essence.

"Hm!" he thought, "could swear that's the sweet stench of something bear-like".

He walked up and down the deck, trying to source a more favourable spot without attracting too much attention. The captain, however, was watching him out of the corner of his eye. Henry had certainly made an impression on him.

"It's much stronger here by the stairs", he thought. But then he was knocked off his feet as the large, double-decked boat, which was already heeling to port given everyone was gathered on the shore-side, was impacted by something large and was threatening to keel over.

"What the hell?" shouted the skipper. "Quick, move over here, all of you," he shouted, holding fast to the wheel and gesturing wildly. "She'll go over if we don't…"

He didn't manage to finish his sentence, as they were hit again, in a similar place. Fortunately, however, whatever the blunt object was applying the force, they had timed the second blow fractionally wrong as the boat had already started righting itself and the weight of the swinging hull counteracted some of the force.

"Bill, is that the sound of splitting?" James had uttered this virtually under his breath as he had moved across to be alongside the skipper, but Henry still heard him.

Despite the outward appearance of calm, Henry could smell the scent of fear coming off the veteran.

"Better get everyone into life jackets, James, just in case," he said, heading for the stairs.

The third bang was followed by a fourth, like two rams hitting in close succession. But this time the boat had been forced into the shallows and was jammed on a group of rocks, effectively beaching it. That at least stopped the rocking but by the now audible tearing and creaking sounds it was clear that the integrity of the hull had been breached.

"Look!" shrieked Lucy, "fins!"

All eyes turned to where she pointed, at the exposed stern of the boat and what looked like two massive, sleek, half-surfaced submarines ploughing through the water towards them. Before anyone could utter another word, both orcas hit in unison and the boat lurched beneath them, well and truly beaching on the shallow rocks.

Anyone who wasn't holding on was thrown to the floor and Bill, who had been halfway down the stairs, was now lying in a heap, unconscious, blood running down his face.

The boat was clearly taking on water now and judging by the area of impact, the propeller was probably out of commission. They were now facing the clearly enraged killer whales on one side and on the other, whatever strange wildlife awaited them on the shore, black bears, cougars and wolves being uppermost on their minds.

The adults were caught in two minds, but before anyone else could act, Savannah was running towards the bow rail. James tried to catch hold of her, but she was much more agile. As he looked up, she was disappearing over the side in a rainbow-hued swallow dive while her family looked on helplessly, in both dread and awe.

S avannah cleared the tail fins of both whales with ease.

But then she spotted that the attack orcas were not alone. The rest of the family pod was circling in the deeper channels, clearly awaiting their call to action. And now they had noticed her.

The air was alive with their unique language of clicks and blows. You didn't have to be a merperson or marine biologist to understand that they were distressed, and something was amiss.

The family of whales fanned out and encircled the brave mermaid, a hunting pattern they employ when looking to first confuse then stun their prey, usually the schools of salmon abundant in this part of the world.

James was comforting himself with the knowledge that there has never been a known killer attack on a human in the wild and that they are very specialist hunters. Even with seals in the area, it is doubtful that this pod would have a taste for anything but fish. Although given Savannah's unique anatomy, that wasn't all that comforting either, especially given this pod wasn't hunting for food but seemed to be bearing a grudge.

"James, we need to get off the boat, it's taking on water, fast."

Elouisa had made her way down the stairs and was tending to the stricken skipper with Holly. "Henry, can you find a ladder or something for us to use, to reach the shallows on the shore side?"

James, Alice and Lucy were now at the seaward side of the boat and could see Savannah in animated conversation with the orca matriarch. This had at least paused the attacks, for now. The two were circling each other in the water while they spoke, which didn't seem to bode well.

"This truce isn't going to last long. There's too many of them and their behaviour is really odd," James muttered, clearly worried.

"I have something we can try, but it relies on the special skills of you two."

Downstairs, Henry picked up the captain effortlessly and accompanied his mother down the rope ladder to the shore. As he stepped over the rail, he noticed that smell again. But this time he couldn't be sure whether it was coming from the boat or, perhaps more worryingly, from the dark woodland fringing the beach.

Savannah was struggling to communicate with the orca matriarch, as she was speaking like a drunken human, her phrases all garbled and aggressively slurred.

As far as she could gather, they believed all humans to be the enemy now and had been instructed by something they called "the source" to remove all craft from their waters.

Savannah had tried to empathise, mentioning the corpses she had seen, but this only seemed to enrage them further as it seems they were related. The only thing stopping them from charging her appeared to be the confusion at her shape beneath the water, as they had seemingly seen several deformed sea-kind lately and they couldn't be sure what exactly the mermaid was. This reminded Savannah of the bizarre shark she had encountered with the dolphins in Mousehole.

"Look," she continued, in her usual soothing way, "we are visitors here. We only arrived recently and were summoned to help."

That, however, seemed to backfire. Fear and distrust of

strangers is an impulse common to most cultures and intelligent cetaceans are no exception, no matter how adversely affected by whatever was infecting their minds.

Suddenly, three of the frustrated juveniles broke from the circle and, despite the warnings from their elders, came at the mermaid in trident formation. Two flanked her while the one in the centre, which had a distinctive missing front tooth, sped up to engage her first.

Savannah didn't have the momentum to take to the air, so she dove instead, the whale passing at least a couple of feet above her, its wake sweeping her flowing hair behind her like a cape.

As she made to deepen her dive, she was blind-sided by the tail of one of the orcas, its camouflage doing its job too well, and next found herself flying through the air.

She twisted as she reached the peak of her arch, spread her arms and managed to combine hang-time with a glide, surfing the air like a flying fish for several metres. This at least ensured that she didn't land in the middle of the rest of the pod.

As she came back down, she pressed the Moonstone at the centre of her necklace and concentrated on the sort of splash-less re-entry an Olympic diver would be proud of. She then veered sharply right, invisible, as the orcas converged on where they guessed she would be.

Undetected, she swam down to the sea grass beds, where several terrified fish were hiding from the predators. They were startled by the current she created but clearly couldn't see her.

Feeling her way through the fronds, she could see the orcas

patrolling the seabed. She had no fear that they would find her, but she was worried they would return to attacking her family on the boat.

Then suddenly, the killer whales scattered. Bizarrely the kelp bed went cold as something huge was blocking out the sun. Savannah looked up and could see something resembling a massive black hybrid between an orca and a great white shark. Its mouth was at least twice the size of the dominant male's and the pod had clearly decided they had met more than their match and were heading out.

There was something about the hybrid abomination that puzzled the mermaid, but just as she was debating her next move, two humanoid shapes broke from the curtain of darkness leading to the deepest part of the channel. They were carrying what looked like a trident, a net and a spear and, incredibly, they appeared to be dark-skinned men with long black hair, tattooed muscular torsos and long, black-blue tails.

"Mermen, here?" uttered Savannah in complete surprise.

The new arrivals headed straight for the composite creature, then split to hit either flank. Both raised their handheld weapons at the same time and lunged simultaneously. But to their clear surprise, their spears simply disappeared into the mass, seemed to encounter no resistance and then were drawn back again. The gash then sealed over instantly.

Trying an alternative approach, the mermen swam to the front of the beast, which seemed to give no sign of their presence. They both then set their weapons to receive, aiming to use the creature's weight and momentum against it. It looked like a crazy plan to Savannah, who was impressed by their bravery, but they were dwarfed by the size of their opponent.

Once again, however, the creature showed no regard for the weapons facing it. It simply tanked straight on, much to the surprise of the warriors.

Savannah could no longer contain herself and called out as the beast engulfed them. She couldn't look and closed her eyes. But when she opened them again, rather than a mess of scales, bone and blood, she was greeted with the sight of two very confused looking mermen, one with a net filled with wriggling dark fish. Then as she approached them, the fish dissolved like a bath bomb.

They didn't have to say anything as their open-mouthed expressions spoke volumes.

Their confusion wasn't helped when they clapped eyes on Savannah's radiant, blonde beauty. But she simply smiled and pointed to the surface, confident in what she would find up there. Sure enough, as they broke the water and took a lungful of white air, first they noticed that there were no signs of fins and second, they were greeted by the broad grin of Lucy, her sister.

Then Alice's head appeared over Lucy's and then finally, her dad's capped the lot.

"Go on then," shouted Savannah. "How did you do it?"

The mermen were initially reluctant to follow Savannah's lead when she swam to the shallows and changed, seamlessly from be-tailed to long-legged as she left the water, clad in a beautiful green-blue dress, the Moonstone radiating like a rainbow.

When they saw Old Bill unconscious on the beach however, they tentatively changed their minds and one of the men was soon walking along the sand, clad in buckskin, soft leather and exotic beads. The other, she noted, seemed to struggle to move on land as if his legs were broken, or worse. Then when she next looked, he had fashioned a crutch from somewhere and had moved, surprisingly swiftly, to join his partner, who had the look of a brother.

The younger girls giggled conspiratorially, however, at the rippling muscles of both men. Alice teased that she had caught a glimpse of a well-toned buttock, which was highly unlikely given how discrete and agile merfolk always are.

There was something about this lithe pair that was both strident and confident but as timid as a wild thing in human company, at the same time.

They reminded Henry of feral wolves.

Alice was explaining to Savannah how Lucy had used the Ravenring to come to her aid. None of them were able to conjure anything large enough to compete with the pod of orcas. So Lucy used the ring to create the illusion of size instead. She conjured up a large shoal of dark fish and, using her gift, formed them into the shape of the mammoth hybrid whaleshark, knowing how the pod would react.

"We had not, however, expected you two," said Alice, in her typically uncompromising way.

"I am Alice, by the way and this is my family. Who are you?"

At first, the stern mermen remained shocked and not a little aloof as she held out her hand. But then their black eyes sparkled, and they burst out laughing.

"The savage spirit warrior is strong in this one," they laughed, taking her hand warmly.

"How did you know that we're Savages?" enquired Lucy, stern-faced, causing everyone to laugh all the harder at her inadvertent joke, until she realised and joined in too.

Soon they were greeting the rest of the family, especially keen to reach Bill, who was finally coming round. Judging by his groans he was facing the inevitable headache as a result of his fall.

The warrior's eyes were whizzing around the group, picking up on all the clues. They lingered over the ancient magic items, noted the demeanour of the family members, the sensitivity of the father, the fact the boy kept his distance and especially how the dark woman barely acknowledged them. A quick glimpse at her dress, signs and ciphers told them all they needed to know.

But having taken their read of the situation, they both kneeled to attend to the skipper.

"You have been in the wars with the sea guardians, old father," joked the broader-shouldered of the two, pressing the large egg on Bill's blackening eye until he winced.

"Press me there again and I swear I'll take that scalp of yours once and for all, Swift Hawk."

They laughed again.

"My brother may have a woman's name and not be able to run like you any longer, but he does not have a gentler touch, as you should know from his beautiful carving."

"Ah, do they not still joke that only the mertribes use his canoes because they mostly travel under the water?"

The brother with the crutch feigned offence, but soon re-launched his smile as they all finally relaxed.

From the moment the scent assaulted Henry's nostrils to shouting the alarm could only have been a split second, but the great bear that suddenly broke from the brush was upon the group before he, or anyone else, could move.

In a bone-shattering second, before the growl even registered, the beast snatched the taller Indian by the shoulder. It shook him violently twice, like a child's rag doll, then threw him to the sand.

It then charged the second.

Instinctively, the disabled brother raised his trident crutch in self-defence. But before the fatal weight of the bear crashed upon him like a muscular wave of fur, Holly launched herself between the man and the animal.

The bear made several aggressive passes with its unsheathed claws, any of which could have split him asunder. But each lunge was frustrated by the scarlet Rubyrobe. The magical cloak seemed to anticipate the animal's planned move before it initiated it.

The angry beast roared and bellowed its frustration, as Holly calmly played matador to the furry aggressor. She barely seemed to move and yet she never took her eyes from those of the wild combatant.

After a short but infuriating dance, the bear changed tactics and appeared to reach out to crush her in an all-embracing hug, intended to pull her head toward its jaws. Yet as it rumbled forward, something landed on its nose and started dancing on its snout. It was Helygenn, the Willowand's altered form. But this time it had morphed into a particularly bulbous and warty toad.

"Ribbet," it belched in the animal's face, causing it to spin and jig on the spot, shaking its head as if it were drenched in spittle. This distracted moment gave Holly and her companion time to withdraw far enough to tend to their stricken friend in relative safety.

Eventually, bored with its game, Helygenn leaped from the bear's snout into the long grass.

By now, however, Alice had transformed and was flying around and around the very confused bear. It was clearly mesmerised by the trail of sparkling stars and the sweet song she sang as she coaxed it away from her family and friends.

However, before the bear disappeared back into the treeline, Henry stepped forward once more, this time in were-form.

His fawn and cream fur caught the late afternoon sun, glinting off the water as he spoke, in finest Brunin, or bear language:

"Mother, please calm yourself. We mean you no harm. We did not intend to disturb your meal. We did not want to raid your larder. And we certainly did not even know that your young one was with us, until now…"

And with this, he stepped to one side and, who should be there but Holly's new friend, Issy.

"I knew I could smell something below," muttered Henry as the bear cub ran at full tilt to her mother.

She stopped, then paused only to shout a last farewell "Oy, I heard THAT. I do have feelings, you know!"

Then both animals melted into the shade of the shoreline trees.

B ack in the cave in Namibia, Moses had been left stranded by the wytch. The portal had now been sealed, somehow.

All energy was drained from the depleted crystal drive. Somebody had also trashed the vehicles, leaving him only one option. He would have to perform a summoning spell.

It had been a very long time since he had embraced the old ways. But he came from sangoma blood, and by making good use of the scant resources about him he managed to find enough totemic touchstone objects to venture an attempt. But first he would need a courier.

Moses had to walk some miles until he found what he was looking for, a tree with a large weaver bird nest. Taking great care, he managed to take one of the females, about set to tend her eggs. He then returned to the cave of all origins, carrying her carefully cradled in his sensitive hands.

"I am sorry, little friend," he whispered to soothe her. "Only one task will I ask of you and then you will be free."

Tentatively, he placed the bird in the centre of the magical circle he had created, before he carefully ignited the series of totemic symbols he had crafted from wood and bone around the circle.

A procession of shadows and shapes reluctantly emerged from each symbol in reply to his rhythmic chants and melted into the form of the bird, taking shape slowly like ideas forming in someone's head. When the last of the embers had died down a mystical firebird bird took one long look at Moses and then took flight.

Moses had an uncomfortable night that night without food or water. But when he woke with the dawn, he heard the unmistakeable sound of horse-kind. A wave of relief passed over him as the sangoma realised that his communication charm had worked out as planned. For, waiting for him outside, were the cavalry, a skittish herd of zebra and they were raring to go,

It took the best part of the long day, galloping through the most intense of the sun's showers, to reach his destination. He alternated between the stallions, yet it was uncomfortable going and he was hugely relieved when they stopped at a watering hole hidden in the rocks that no man would ever have seen.

The person Moses sought was manning her store, seemingly in the middle of nowhere, at the side of a dirt road that no more than half a dozen cars passed in a week.

Isla Biddu was a striking looking woman in orange robes and the distinctive yellow headdress of her tribe. She was the head of a female cooperative of mystical artisans who made and sold curios including dolls, sewn goods, semi-precious stones and key rings made from animal hide. As expected, she barely batted an eyelid at the manner of his arrival, although he would hardly have known, given she was sporting a pair of mirrored aviator glasses. She also barely broke sentence as, when he arrived on his unconventional steed, she was mid-way through a long conversation with her Windhoek agent, talking on a state-of-the-art mobile phone boosted by a satellite dish on the roof of her modest shop.

B ack at Tofino, news had already started to spread about the
near disaster that beset Captain Bill and his English
customers.

So by the time they had hitched a ride with the mermen's tribe,
the Salish people, there was quite the reception committee
waiting.

The Rubyrobe had worked its healing magic during the
journey, during which they all learned that their two new friends
were also known as Bear and Swift Hawk.

Before the family could object, they were wrapped in
distinctive Hudson Bay native blankets and gathered together
round a large table. Soon they were enjoying warm bowls of
delicious chowder at the famed Schooner restaurant, a charming
place in the bay, in the distinctive shape of a boat.

The friendly eatery gave them an excellent view over the town
and the Pacific Ocean, as it folds around Clayoquot Sound, the
lively body of river. All appeared calm and tranquil once again.

But one of the group knew how to read the signs of the forest and shoreline well. And judging by the shapes Henry could see in the water and the hubbub of the gathering crowds, it was clear that several angry orca pods were now patrolling the area. Above the surface all seemed fine. But in the water, something in nature's balance was still clearly very, very unstable.

D eep in the back woods, where the forest is like a living maze with fronds, frosts and fogs clutching at the strange, something wicked walked slowly but relentlessly, alone.

Barely a sound had the shape made; black was its aura and its essence so malign. Yet in the domain of the wild cat and the bandit-faced racoon, the stranger was soon news. For here, every step taken was something disturbed, a message sent to the quiet spirits that guard this place. Breathing in the damp mist was like whispering and muttering in the sea breeze, sent signals for listening senses to hear.

The unwitting would mistake this place for lifeless. But Cougar-Annie, who famously carved out a life in this terrain, knew well what lurked beneath the leaf litter and lichen; the paw print of the predator, child-stealer and breath-taker. And it was toward Annie's ramshackle wooden home that the stranger drifted, floating through the foliage with the certainty of one born to the place, not recently arrived from the other side of the globe as this wretched soul had.

The sensitive crone could also hear the slightest shift in the detritus that littered the forest floor, the intake of breath others obsessed with their own thoughts would miss. So she knew they were there long before they saw or smelt her, a noxious blend of old blood, bat, bone and bad intentions.

Despite her lonely appearance, which gave the dark-robed figure the illusion of vulnerability, the shadowy aura that followed her like a personal storm was subtly charged with ancient lore and a sharp malevolence that stank of spite. This meant she proceeded, unmolested, along the rough path, although opportunities for ambush were plenty.

Perhaps the predators of Boat Basin on this part of Clayoquot Sound had been conditioned by hard-earned tough experience to understand that sinewy and snaggle-toothed women as old and tough as vintage leather were best given a wide berth? For it was fearfully whispered around these parts, that the skeletons of over fifty cougars and four husbands attested to the quiet power of the malevolent matriarch who had infamously worn her disappointments on her skin, like tracks in the sand.

As the crone breached the tree canopy and oozed out into a glade, suddenly the flora started to change. Here, the plant life subtly took on a more cultivated and half-cultured look. Where once traps and snares lurked in wait at fence lines, now primary-coloured plants and flowers danced. These ancient seed beds were testimony to the founding resident's vision and attempts to civilise and tame the wild. She had tried but failed, just.

But this traveller had no interest in flora, sentiment or the trivia of pioneers. She respected little but her own wretched obsessions and was made of more primal stuff. In fact, as she cut through the long grass, the shrubs withered either side of her, their colours first bleeding and then fading to dusty beige. Snakes slithered hastily from her path. Soon, a wake of twisted stems and drooping heads parted behind her, cutting an abused path through the islands, a trail of uncharacteristic destruction.

This blow-in traveller was drawn here, not by the civilising schemes of the founding mother, but by the aura of conquest and indomitability. The arcane energy and dark craft that saw Annie outlast every one of her weaker mates, and some of her children too, was still in this misty air. But the secret of exactly how many fed the worms here went to the grave with her. It is not for nothing that it is still claimed that the cries of Annie's dead children can be heard on the winter wind.

This wytch had deliberately ported to be near this very spot, where the earth was soaked in blood, sweat and sorrow. For here, the very roots reeked of someone who refused to go meekly at the dying of the sun or of the light.

The wiccan essence was powerful in this wildly desolate place of decay and re-birth, of shade and deeper shade, layers of pastoral witchery. And that was the primeval power source she needed now to push forward her ancient fight. For there was dark work to be done here still, malign craft indeed.

As she set foot on the creaking stoep of bleached, cracked and buckled pine, it was fitting that from across the water, two wolves howled to herald the night. Then as the wizened one entered the ancient house, a rocking chair creaked as if someone or something had woken.

Book 2:
Spirit Animals

She heard something almost sigh, then rustle in the bushes, signifying a move, and had to stifle a scream, her eyes flicking up to her grandfather's, who had just seen it too.

There, on the trunk of a tree, was what appeared to be a family group of animals. Well, parts of animals. They were animal skeletons, in fact. And as they looked, Lucy could swear that they were gradually, determinedly coming to life.

The Tofino natives were twitching with restlessness. These were tough people. Never, in living memory had all their boats been grounded and so suddenly. And for such sea-faring folk, it was like losing a sense or a limb.

It was worse still for those reliant on commercial trade and visitors, as people came here for the water and the joys of the sea.

While the unseasonal volume of orca traffic was certainly novel and their erratic behaviour drew the crowds, the impact of watching from the shore soon waned. Rumours spread of houses built over the sea sustaining damage from the killer whales, of kayakers dragged under, fearing for their lives and of tourists choosing to move on to safer towns for their fishing, ocean-based activity and sight-seeing tours.

There were still a few more reckless, thrill-seeking types who wanted to take to the ocean, as there always are. But when one veteran in a speedboat was attacked only a few yards from the port jetty and barely managed to escape with all his limbs intact, people started thinking twice. The jetty was badly damaged by a frenzied pod, so the police stepped in and, despite protests, officially shut down the whole of the bay.

Angry town council meetings were being held daily to try and get to grips with the problem. Animal behaviourists and marine biologists were brought over from the mainland. But there was little anyone could do because they were not able to access the animals in the bay and they had nothing to compare this problem to, no reference points, no data. Nobody had seen aggressive behaviour of this nature on this scale before.

That night, to this chaotic backdrop, the family gathered around the fire to unpack what had happened to them since they had landed. Brinn, who had been quietly soaking up events and had been consulting the local sages, was holding court in his usual, calm but cracking voice.

"According to the tribal elders, this has only happened once before. And as far as I can tell, it coincided with some dark magical storm that had such a devastating impact on the people of this area that they deserted the land for several generations."

This got the family's attention, as they were still assembling all the pieces of their own story in the right order, and each week seemed to bring fresh revelations.

"I understand there is a great mountain range that starts beneath the ocean. The local people call it the hill of fire or Firehill."

This earned a noticeable intake of breath from the children who were only too familiar with that word.

"They say that the gods live there, and it glows when they are angered. The tip of an ancient volcano is known as the stove pipe or chimney, a vent in the Firehills. It is incredibly strong here as it is so close to the original volcanic source."

He paused and sipped from a glass of beer.

"This is the pressure release for the magma, or molten lava in the entire mountain range both above and below the water. It is believed to be the breath of the ancient gods."

He smiled at this point.

"Our merman friends have volunteered to take me to what they call the Cloud Mountain. They believe this, if anywhere, may be where the problems started. But it is the territory of a renegade band of Mohawk, eternal enemies of the water tribes. That means this trip is not going to be an easy one."

"So now for the surprise news," said Elouisa, sarcastically. "Never let it be said this family ever takes the soft option, eh?"

"But you know that something else has changed here. We have all felt it," her husband replied.

"Yes," answered Brinn, "that is why we must move fast, for SHE has come, as we knew she would, and it is said that she will only be here for the one reason."

With perfect timing, much to his clear shock, James' cell phone started to buzz, and he excused himself. It was Moses, confirming what they had suspected about the sea wytch and confirming their worst fears too.

"That woman is nothing. if not relentless in her evil," he said, as he came off the Face Time call.

"Moses has had a torrid time of it. Looks like we now need to get cracking even sooner than planned, for Moses is not able to track her exact whereabouts. She has drained the portal crystals to cover her tracks." His children's faces told their own weary story about their feelings for the malevolent matriarch.

"For all we know, she could well be at the site already. He believes she intends to use the power of the volcano to multiply the pace and range of the dark poison, her organic spell. The portal allows her to access the Firehills as far as the ancient range extends above and below the water to the places where the very continents join. If she succeeds in poisoning..." his voice trailed off, "...if she does, well, before we can blink, half this continent will move over to darkness and blight. Then the next. Then..."

So, gathering close lest prying ears were listening, the next stage in the defence plan was hatched in a huddle.

A hunter squad was established to try and track her down. Their role was also to see what could be done about finding an antidote for the current mental illness besetting the killer whale community. For this Savannah, Lucy and Swift Hawk were to work with Elouisa and Brinn, who would find lengthy, speedy travel a struggle.

James and Bear were to lead the other party. They were to trek, at speed, to the Firehills. Henry, Holly and Alice were to help too, the girls providing stealth air cover while Henry's unique skills were to be employed to enlist some local help, guided by their friend from the first people.

As the family members quietly set about the business of readying themselves for this latest challenge, James and Elouisa had a moment of mutual pride, where their eyes met above the bustle of their family and friends.

How far this incredible group of people had come on their journey of re-connection. How much they had achieved together, absorbing and adapting to challenges thrown at them. But how much stronger would they have to become to finally throw off the shackles of sickness, narcissism, selfishness and spite that had been dragging them beneath the waves of sadness for far too long now?

The wolf pack serenading the rising moon had been the custodians of this territory for as long as their ancient ancestral line implied. Their elders knew every rock and tree and moss bed. and they were either feared or respected by every living creature in this realm.

Even the aggressive, rugged and hardy pioneers or first settlers knew to keep their distance. And wisely, the wolves had found a way of accommodating man, steering clear of their children and animals. In return, the wood clearers did not venture into the heart of their range, their ancient home.

Naturally, it was this pack who were the first to detect the change in the weather, the water and the scents on the wind that caused the problems now facing the guardians of the deep.

The worlds of wolf and whale rarely overlap. For the water is too sharp and cold and strong ever to tempt them, and sightings of the black and white guardians on land were few and very far between.

But today, Ice Eye, the matriarch, was advised that she was

needed at the table stone by the shore.

She arrived, flanked by her alpha brothers, both as black as night, to a strange scene.

There, part-beached on the rock, was a huge bull orca, looking as cumbersome as a pup atop a tree. But what was altogether stranger was that, judging by the skids and scrapes, this beaching had been deliberate.

The three wolves walked slowly, cautiously round to the front of the ocean guardian and were carefully pondering what to say and how, when a large crow alighted upon a branch above the orca.

"Thank you for coming. I am the herald, and behold, the king of the southern pod from Telegraph Bay. He has appointed me to speak for him, as he needs your help."

It appeared that the sharp-eyed crow was translating subtle clicks and audible vents from the blowhole, like someone playing a woodwind instrument.

"He has travelled to this territory because he has heard of the problems of his kind and believes that they are being poisoned by something foul entering the water here in the sound. He believes it is a form of liquid evil gripping his kind and he fears that, if left unchecked, it will soon spread to the beasts of the land."

Ice Eye remained impassive in the teeth of this speech, not out of rudeness, but because she was taking everything in. Crows in these parts have a reputation for trickery and she had learned not to give trust too fast.

She recalled being sung a tale about a magical crow from the time of her grandparents, crows often communing with and speaking for different realms and worlds, including that of the dead. So, while unusual, she was not entirely shocked by this strange scene.

"If this were true, night-treader, then why bring this news to me? Does he seek to start a war with the two-footed, pink fleshed humans? Does he know how strong they are and the mechanical magic they possess? Such war would not end well."

"No," she answered. "He does not believe this is the fault of the humans. He too is concerned that they are becoming afeared of his kind and he dreads the backlash if there is a fatal attack on the soft skinned ones."

The whale, at this point, splashed the shallows behind in order to sprinkle what water he could on his skin, fast drying even under this weak sun.

"With respect, what can we do to help?"

"Ah!" said the crow with a cackled cough of a voice. "You wolves like to head straight for the moot point, I see. Well, it is known that you sometimes commune with the ancient people, the travelling tribes. He was hoping you could find a way, somehow, to make your fears known when next you are called upon to dance through their dreams."

The wolf was taken aback at this reference to the spirit creature ceremony, the most ancient of communal arts where the Indian elders morphed with a chosen totemic animal and they ran or flew or swam together.

"I can see your surprise, m'lady. But do I have to remind you that, as slight and useless as we seem, a whole human tribe of some nobility called themselves after us, the Crow."

The wolf couldn't help but smile at the whale companion's legendary sensitive ego.

"So, if they do hold a ceremony of summoning, as they sometimes do at this year time, what exactly do we say to them in order to sort this out?"

"Well, whether they do and if they choose to summon the spirit of the wolf, we need you to explain that we are not the source of the problem. We also need them to quest to track down the poison, for only the humans have the power to go against nature and put things right."

The wolf leader nodded sagely, signalling understanding.

"I can see that you have a plan of at least some sense. But what if they don't know what to do?"

"Well," said the crow, interpreting the whale again, "We also need you to set a number of packs to go searching for the source, for my friend here is unfortunately rather challenged in the feet department."

This joke clearly amused the crow, but her croaking laughter only lasted a few seconds before the steely gaze of the she-wolf murdered her mirth.

"Even though that quest will probably mean reaching beyond your ancestral range."

"Now THAT could cause a problem, as you know that the realm of the cougar is not a safe place for us. They resent what they see as a collaboration between us and the humans and will hit us hard."

"We are aware," said the crow. "But we have little or no choice, as this matter will soon become critical. Dangerous people will come if the sound cannot be productive. If that happens, many creatures will pay the price, not just the whales."

The wolf went quiet again, then smiled.

"But surely that carnage, like all battles, would only suit the crows?"

The herald went quiet for a while and then replied.

"Well, it does appear that for once, this is a win/win for corvid-kind."

"As ever," smirked the wolf, licking her paw absent-mindedly, then turning and walking slowly away.

Sensing their parlez over, the giant orca gave one last bellowing exhale and started to wriggle his huge torso back toward the sea. His kind could tolerate the land, but it was obvious it was not their natural domain.

"What was his final word?" the she-wolf requested.

"Oh, nothing too important. Let's just say he urges you to hurry up."

And with that, the whale finally slid back into the water and hauled itself through the shallows to the deeper channels, while the crow called farewell and took to the air.

"I shall be back to lend a hand," the crow called, as it took to the grey sky.

"I am Nubia, by the way," she called, with a series of "caw, caws".

"And I feel compelled to say that, despite all I have said, I have a very bad feeling about this."

Travel by water was not thought to be an option until Old Bill called round, unexpectedly.

Such was the coincidence of his arrival to find them packing supplies, that a suspicious soul would suspect that he had somehow got wind of their challenges.

Whatever the reason for his appearance, he was a welcome sight. His proposal was very welcome too.

Repairs to the boat were complete and Bill had been working all night to place reinforcement around the hull and install some counter measures to deter the whales.

"If we launch from my home slipway, we should be far enough down channel not to trouble the patrolling pods," he announced confidently.

"It will be much easier, from the water, to make several beach stops and cover a lot more ground. Hell, we should be able to search all the way from here down past Cougar-Annie's haunted garden to No'otka Island if we head at first light."

James was in two minds about the risks, but Brinn and Elouisa's eyes lit up at the prospect.

"We have support in the ocean if need be and we won't be straying too far from the shore, darling," she said, half reassuringly.

"Will Henry be coming with us?" asked Bill, rather surprising them.

"Not this time. We need our champ with us," announced James, putting his arm around the old man's shoulders. But he noticed father and son exchange some sort of knowing look, that he hadn't time to unpack.

"If things go according to plan, we'll be meeting back here soon enough, with a chance to finally relax into something like a holiday."

But as the words left James's mouth, he realised that virtually the entire history of this changeling family had been a perpetual journey; always travelling, exploring but very little time spent together, settling, arriving. He did wonder to himself when the quest would end or, with a heavy heart, whether that was destined to be their fate.

After launching the Okhawo, they were all a little tense with the slow-going, traversing the currents to first reach the opposite beach to land half their number. Despite their nerves, there was no sign of the whales so far, only a large school of cod, sheltering down channel to escape the predators up near Tofino Sound.

The away island party of James, Holly, Alice, Henry and Bear were soon saying their goodbyes and heading off along the track, the native merman taking point.

Meanwhile, Old Bill turned the blue and silver boat around, deciding to hug this shore for a while, before re-crossing in more stable waters slightly further down the coast.

The girls were happy to don their faerie forms, a transformation Bear simply took in his stride as if it were an everyday occurrence (he was fae-kind too, after all).

The fluttering duo headed high into the tree canopy for a better vantage point. They were merrily flying literal bright rings around each other with aerial gymnastics, when Holly remembered that the raptors in these parts were unknown to them, and they in turn knew very little about their loyalties or knowledge of European faeries.

So they opted for discretion instead and stifled, with some difficulty, the giggling, sparkles and fireworks mid-flight.

From the top of the trees, they could see all the way back up to the town. There was no obvious path ahead, so the girls were impressed by their guide's bush skills in somehow finding their way.

Having stretched their flying muscles, the glamorous duo decided to weave between the tips of the trees high above the heads of their party.

Back on the rainforest floor, meanwhile, the group had broken into a modest jog. Henry was clearly having to restrain himself from unleashing the beast within. Bear was no slouch on land, it seemed, although James was feeling the burn and compensating by appearing to ride, unbeknown to the others, on the carved staff he had brought along from the house, for walking. It was shaped like a sinuous snake and he commanded it with ease. The warlock just had one buttock on the staff and his feet were almost both touching the leaf litter as they flew past.

Henry was starting to pant, quite audibly, and itching round his neck. The rainforest humidity and dense vegetation wasn't helping his self-control much, nor were the enticing sights, sounds and smells surrounding them.

The route took the party along fallen tree trunks at times, leaping trickling streams and clumps of hart's tongue fern. They must have been going for almost an hour when Bear suddenly paused by the trunk of a mighty maple and fell to his haunches. He had his hand to his mouth indicating the need for silence. But unfortunately, the air force hadn't seen the signal. They were giggling about something a swarm of midges had said to Alice after she nearly singed them with sparks as she passed through.

Henry suddenly threw his nose into the air, his senses filled with the musk of an apex predator.

Somewhere, very close by, a mountain lion or cougar had been hunting. And as Henry flicked his head to the left, he caught the fawn and black tip of a thick tail disappearing into a mossy clump of rocks and tree roots.

He made as if to move in that direction but then caught the disapproving expression of their guide who gestured with his palm that they must continue the opposite way. There was clearly little chance of communing with the phantom of the forest now. There were too many of them to earn anything like the trust they would need. So they set off on their trek again, at the same steady pace.

They had travelled for a fair few more miles and Henry still had the sour smell of big cat in his nostrils. In fact, it seemed to be growing stronger and he could feel himself starting to change in response. His pulse was increasing, sinews popping and senses sharpening. His fangs were cutting the inside of his mouth and bottom lip where the tension was felt the strongest.

The wereboy scanned the undergrowth on both sides of the rough path but could detect no sign, and now the scent was changing, morphing. It was as obvious as a switch from cat to devil dog.

"Wolves," he muttered under his breath. "And many of them, a pack at least." He considered warning the others but wanted to be sure.

Then, as they rounded a large, moss-encrusted outcrop of rock nestled between a row of ancient trees, a loud snarl brought the party to a sudden stop. For there, barring the way, atop the trunk of a fallen pine which had become lodged against another, creating a platform twenty feet in the air, was not one but three magnificent cougars. And unusually for their kind, as they are solitary, ambush predators, they were calling the humans out, as a pack, spoiling for a fight.

"Cats in wolf territory," said Henry. "There must be something giving them the foolhardiness to trespass in this way."

"Yes," said Bear. "This is deep in the territory of the Grey Tail pack, and for them to stand up to humans in this way suggests they are disturbed. Perhaps the disease of the orcas has spread to land?"

As he said this, he manoeuvred to ensure that the adults had eyes on both flanks as well as before and behind them.

The large, lithe, tan-coloured cats now fanned out. They were normally solo hunters but seemed adept at team tactics, something their distant African cousins excel at.

One thing they could not have accounted for, however, was the existence of air cover. As their party members set spear and staff to receive a charge, and Henry transformed fully into were-kind, the girls flew down to an effective height.

As the Willowand started to stir in anticipation of some action, however, Holly spotted shapes shifting in the undergrowth. They were encircling the position below and slowly tightening a living net of muscle, teeth and fur.

"This should be interesting," whispered Alice, in response to Holly's nudge. "But what if they're not friendly either?"

"Oh, I think we know who they're more interested in, don't we?"

Henry's senses were now alive with multiple targets. There was so much activity around them that he didn't know which way to turn.

"Wolves now," he hissed as a warning, but just as he did, a collective snarl hit them like a wave.

The power of the pack overwhelmed the cougars who were taken by complete surprise, such was their focus on the humans. Leaves, shrubs and soil was flying, fur as well. It only took a few seconds of frantic conflict before the large cats scrambled for refuge in the deeper forest.

Leaving his soldiers to finish the job and give chase the length of the pack's territory, the alpha male approached Bear. He was clearly pleased to see him.

"Greetings, Long Tooth," said Bear, bowing slightly. "How is your queen?"

"She is well, thank you. The winter was less harsh than the worst years. But right now, she is meeting with the ocean guardians to discuss the troubles."

"I see the troubles, as you call them, have come onto the land too."

"You mean those ghosts of the woods?" she nodded in the direction of the fleeing cougars, who clearly didn't fancy the 3:1 odds.

"Well, they do appear to be a deal more desperate. They have never been known to hunt like their cousins, the savannah lions. These are normally solitary beasts. But it's a bit early to blame their bold actions on what has poisoned the orcas. Despite the mild weather, food has been scarce this fallow season, my friend, as you know."

At this, the girls descended to a lower branch to get a better look at the handsome pack leader.

"And if we had to rely on brightly-coloured buzzards or hummingbirds to survive, well I'm sure we would all soon go mad."

Alice turned to her sister and whispered.

"He meant us, didn't he? How dare…"

But Holly shut her down with a smile, as she could see Pops moving forward.

"My apologies for being so rude and not introducing myself. I am not catching every word as my Druid language skills are not what they should be but I…"

Long Tooth, however, saved him the long explanation as he turned his head and announced:

"You are the people of the Totem. You are the legend incarnate. You are the spirit in the flesh," he announced, as if they words had been chanted many times before. And this," he said, rounding on Henry, "is the one we are here for today."

The way he worded that last sentence raised the hackles on Henry's back, and he instinctively fell onto all four limbs. His body had gone into some sort of unconscious remote control and he found that he was squaring his shoulders and drawing back his lips to reveal the whiteness, strength and size of his were-fangs. He didn't want to strike this pose, but instinct was taking over.

"Um, Henry…" said James, pointing both of his palms to the floor in a gesture to diffuse the mounting tension.

But instead, a noise like a bubbling volcano started to rise from Henry's chest, and he could now see fresh saliva pooling around his incisor teeth.

"HENRY…"

But there was nothing James could say that could stop what had been set in motion by the laws of nature, it seemed, as his son advanced slowly on the pack leader, not taking his eyes off him for a second.

James tried to cover his own exposed back, edging towards a tree and gripping his snake staff slightly tighter. He was pleased that the girls were in the tree canopy.

Bear had not moved at all. He simply assumed his spectator role; impassive watching nature unfold.

Long Tooth stood his ground. He appeared even larger, were that possible, and seemed rooted to his space. But he was neither provoking nor retreating from Henry's advance.

The pack, however, were slowly tightening the circle and

everywhere you looked were low-slung eyes, teeth and parting leaves and fronds, but barely a sound.

Advancing, paw before paw, muscle before bulging sinew, Henry came to within a couple of feet from Long Tooth's impassable jaws, when something broke from the trees behind them and barked a command in lupine language which James didn't quite understand.

This was clearly the alpha female, and much to the warlock's eternal relief, she had just commanded the pack to stand down. Instantly, to a wolf, they sank to their stomachs. All, that is, bar Long Tooth, who remained alert. The matriarch's mate's body language remained unwaveringly indomitable. But when his son finally let his cold gaze drop, James felt the sweat on his own back tingle.

I ce Eye wasn't just named for her bi-coloured pupils, one hazel and one blue. Her calm and cool control over the Clayoquot pack was the stuff of legend. She was the much-needed salve to her partner's fiery personality.

"You are lucky I arrived when I did, Bear," she joked, as they walked side by side down the path to their den.

"He has always wanted to test his strength against one of the mixed-breeds."

She spoke the last bit quietly, not wishing to re-inflame a delicate situation with a controversial phrase.

"It has been a while since changelings have graced these shores. Well, not since..."

"Um, you forget something, your grace."

"Of course. I am sorry, friend. This is the second time today that I have been reminded that I must be more mindful of the link between the land and the ocean domains."

She then brought Bear up to speed with events at the altar rock.

James, meanwhile, had managed to talk Henry into morphing

back to his alternate form, which he did, reluctantly. This did seem to diffuse much of the tension, although the wolves were only slightly more comfortable, given the uneasy truce that exists between their kind and humans in these and other parts.

He had signalled to the girls, however, that they should stay aloof and out of reach where they were. There was much about this situation that had him very much on edge, given they were deep in the territory of the pack and heavily outnumbered.

The route to the den was understandably complicated and involved lots of twists and turns and diversions through what looked like impenetrable places. But for those in the know, it was navigated without thought.

What was most unexpected was the walk behind a beautiful waterfall, a feature not listed on any area maps, as part of an ancient agreement to keep the peace between humans and wolves. It was the other side of this cascade that the fantasy world unfolded.

The flipside of the falls seemed to have its own micro-climate. It was noticeably warmer but fresher here and the dappled sunshine peeping through the leaf canopy seemed to be a permanent feature. From their vantage point, it reminded the girls of Ashridge, especially Alice who found herself thinking of her other home, the glade.

"It's beautiful," said Holly, pointing to the crèche of cubs, lively balls of feisty fluff.

They raced as fast as tiny paws would allow to greet the returning warriors, no doubt hoping for a solid meal as well. They now wrestled and tussled with each other, competing for the attention of the adults.

A series of caves in a solid wall of rock marked one boundary of the den, while the other sides consisted of a dense bank of trees leading down to a very rocky promontory out to the wildest part of the ocean. The wolves had chosen well, for this special place was only accessible from one side and that only by single file along a concealed ledge.

"They do find it tricky returning with prey," said a voice from an unseen source, in another tree.

It was the crow from the altar rock conference.

"Most inconsiderate for my people who do rely so on our mammalian friends for scraps."

The sisters froze, not sure what to say, given their subterfuge had been so suddenly overturned.

"Don't worry, your secret is safe with me. Been a while since I've seen faerie-kind. Smaller than I recall," she crowed, mischievously.

"Allow me to introduce myself, I am Nubia." She bowed her shining, obsidian black head slightly.

"I was recently appointed consul on behalf of the new animal alliance and I'm getting to grips with our new friends, as it seems are you also."

The girls flew over to the same branch, introduced themselves and soon confided as much of their story since arriving in Canada as they felt wise. They focused on the odd behaviour of some of the animals and their problem-solving role, as that appeared to be what they all had in common.

"So you say something similar has happened in Britain and in Africa? And this map, you mention, now suggests that the Americas may be the ultimate source?" They nodded.

"Fascinating," she replied in a sage tone, almost owl-like in her mannerisms. "While others here have only just started noticing, largely because humans are now affected, we corvids have detected a marked change in patterns of behaviour of the orcas, especially when they hunt, where they go and how they...." she paused before finishing, "...taste."

The girls looked at each other. But the crow pressed on to deflect from the delicate subject.

"What with all the beachings, we carrion crows have had quite a boon," she said, then realised she had made things worse.

"But the good news is, it only seems to have affected the killer whales so far."

"And the cougars", Holly suggested, alluding to their earlier encounter.

"Well, yes, that was odd. But then that may have been something else, or maybe it was because they have feasted on the beach carrion too..."

Then she realised what she was saying and stuttered to a stop.

"But if that affected the cougars, surely it means that the crow-kind will soon..." Holly too realised what Nubia had realised a split-second before.

"I'm sure nothing will come of it. There must be another explanation for the cougars," offered Holly, awkwardly.

Alice, meanwhile, just looked on, open-mouthed.

The alpha pair soaked up the ritual deference of their pack who scented, snickered and supplicated themselves before them, reinforcing ancient bonds and order.

While Bear was warmly greeted as well, it was noticeable that James and Henry were largely ignored or actively avoided.

"I am sorry for the absence of warmth, but I am sure you understand that our kind were once trapped and shot for bounty and our very skins by your kind, from the time they first stole our lands and upset the pact here."

James smiled indulgently at Ice Eye's explanation, but it still didn't make relaxing any easier.

"I am sorry to press," he replied, "and rest assured we do not wish to intrude, but we are only here because we were led to believe that your pack may be able to shed some light on the source of the troubles. Our mission is to restore balance if we can, not make matters worse."

He made sure he was holding the she-wolf's gaze as he said this. This was not intended as an act of aggression, which he knew prolonged eye contact could be interpreted as by wolf-kind, but to assure her of his integrity and the seriousness of his point.

He then looked away, then back again, initiating a response.

"I do see the sincerity in your words, James. And by your leave, we will consult with Bear, who we know from ancient bonds, and we will return with our considered response. Please do relax, if you can, with your changeling son. He appears to need a father's reassurance right now."

Henry was, indeed, very tense, for reasons he didn't fully understand. So it was a relief when they were ushered, by their Indian guide, to a mirror-clear bathing pool, heated, it appeared, by volcanic gas.

"Well, Henry, nothing like a relaxing bath to wash away the grime of the trail."

So the two stripped down and entered the soothing water. They were certainly glad to nibble on the nuts and berries they were offered, although notably neither touched the parcels of jerky-style dried meat.

By the time the pair had dressed again, the counsel had dissolved, and Bear approached them with the outcome. By the look on his face, not everything had gone according to plan and he took James to one side to explain.

"The wolves do not believe that it is coincidental that the problems have occurred at the time of your arrival. They are especially afraid of your son, for reasons I do not understand, given we too are changelings of a tribe they know well. But then wolves are, by nature, highly distrustful.

"They have offered us a form of protection. But they will not be seen to be running with us. We have passage through their territory, which is good news as it extends to most of the area we will visit.

"They have also suggested we search an ancient overgrown camp that once housed a now extinct tribe. They believe this disease came once before and there may be clues there."

James was relieved that they at least had something to go by and a way forward, of sorts. But he was saddened that they had failed to earn the trust of the pack leaders. He did, however, understand their skittishness. Many things in their world were in precarious balance.

So, after a refreshing and enlightening stop-over in the Waterwall Den, during which the sisters had also managed to learn much from their new acquaintance, they were all heading off into the ample bosom of the forest again. This time they were searching for something that may well be at the heart of the mystery that had followed them to three continents.

As their march picked up the pace, they didn't know whether to be disturbed or reassured by evidence of being followed into the spectral shade.

But it wasn't long before the rhythm of the running cast their minds across the water, to where the other half of the family were on their own unique odyssey, running risks as great as those they faced.

There were still no aggressive encounters on the water, much to the relief of all aboard. They had all been on edge during both crossings of Clayoquot Sound. They must have been far enough upstream not to come to the attention of the pods policing the sound, whatever their reason.

Savannah and Swift had taken to the water for the return trip, hoping to act as an early warning and distraction should the orcas come. Secretly, it also gave them the chance to get to know each other beneath the waves, where they were both at their best.

She was instantly struck by her Indian companion's well-honed physique and powerful swimming style. His colours were a blend of burgundy and black contrasting with her greens and blues. For his part, he had frankly never seen such grace and guile in a mermaid and was beguiled by her charms.

Up on the surface, Brinn had stripped an elder sapling of a couple of branches. He was fashioning something that looked like a divining rod.

Elouisa had suggested that Bill stay with the beloved boat. But he had given her a look that suggested he had other plans. Lucy too had insisted that he come along, having grown very accustomed to his reassuring presence.

Bill gave her a smile as he lugged their mini rucksacks from the deck, also handing out water bottles "just in case". Then last of all, he slung a rifle over his shoulder.

This made Elouisa wince a little, given the changelings in their band, but she thought twice about protesting.

Soon, they too were hacking inland; Bill and his Indian friend, who moved ably despite his crutch and crippled leg, leading the way, and Brinn taking the rear, holding the two bent branches in front of him like a couple of handguns made from wire. Oddly, everyone just took this eccentric behaviour in their stride, saying nothing.

"Can someone give me some idea what or why exactly we're looking for, folks? The most obvious geology is across the sound, where the hills descend into the sea. Over here, like on this island, all we're likely to find are old settlements and the odd broken saw or ruptured plough. Folks settled this shoreline first, y'see."

Elouisa could tell that they were going to have to come clean about their nemesis the sea wytch at some point, as her plan to shake Bill off at the boat had backfired. So, as they picked their way through the lush landscape, over tree roots like elephant trunks and lichen-encrusted boulders like tribes of stone trolls, she decided to take Bill into their confidence. In whispers, she gave him the abridged version of their recent story.

A man of many adventures himself, he was surprisingly

understanding, barely shocked and not at all judgemental. He also asked few questions,

"When you live so close to nature, so far from cities and major towns, as we do, you learn to accept a lot and to keep an open mind about the ancient ways," he whispered to the cloaked woman watching him closely, reading his signs.

As he did, he noticed the attractive antique dagger she now had strapped to her belt, the hilt much more ornately carved than his Bowie woodsman's knife.

Before he could ask her about it, a cry came from the rear.

"This way, we need to divert over here." It came from the old man who was now pointing with his forehead in the direction in which both the twigs in his palms had suddenly lurched.

Quickly, their native companion used his crutch, which seemed oddly sharp and magically light in his hands, to fight a way through the thick growth of creepers slung between the trees. Despite his strength, they took some shifting, proving that nobody had used this route for some time.

Once the merman had created a large enough gateway, he accompanied Brinn through. Bill dropped to the back and the ladies were sandwiched between.

They could still make out the semblance of a once well-trodden path. But the tree canopy had sealed over, preventing much growth on the ground. It was also noticeably cooler here.

Working their way in the man-sized space beneath a mighty fallen tree, they came into a clearing that reminded Lucy of the scene in Bambi, where the deer grazed just before tragedy struck and the hunters shot his mother. And sure enough, on the far side of the tranquil glade, a group of deer were grazing. They had yet to spot the companions, which suggested they were not accustomed to encountering people in this safe place.

As the group slowed to a halt and drank in the scene, Brinn noticed that the rods were on the move again. They slowly and hauntingly rotated through 180 degrees back in the direction they had just come.

Lucy noticed this too and she found her eyes moving from the deer to the sticks and then back to the tree trunk they had just walked under.

As she did this, she heard something almost sigh, then rustle in the bushes, signifying a move and she had to stifle a scream, her eyes flicking up to her grandfather's, who had just seen it too.

Now, on the trunk of a tree, was what appeared to be a family group of animals. Well, parts of animals. They were animal skeletons, in fact. And as they looked, Lucy could swear that they were gradually, determinedly coming to life.

"Run!" shouted Swift Hawk, who raised his crutch like a weapon and placed himself between the family and the monsters in one fluid movement. "That way." He was pointing across the glade, where the deer had just fled.

Bill and Brinn, however, were hardly the sprinting kind.

Picking his target carefully, the Indian engaged with what looked like the skeleton of a mountain lion, judging by its shape and length. His thrusts with the crutch were snapping vertebrae, but he was struggling to disable it, given that it was an awkward target. The fanged end, however, snapped and clacked toward his face.

Another cougar zombie was circling round and going for the women. A big mistake, however, as Elouisa smashed it to dust with a single blow from the enchanted Athame. The dagger was proving especially effective against unnatural and demonic beasts. Brinn chose a different tactic. He was still commanding and directing the two sticks but they were now whirling through the air like helicopter propellers. These rampant strimmer blades made short work of a group of what looked like rodent remains, including a snaggle-toothed otter, their animated bones spinning back through the glade or crumbling to dust.

Bill, on the other hand, made it half-way across the open ground before his way was blocked by an abomination rising from what appeared to be a patch of swamp or a tar pit. It stood around six feet at the shoulder, had a very large skull, claws and teeth and a clearly aggressive intent.

He fired two swift shots from his hunting rifle at it, shooting from the hip, but one sailed straight through the bones while the second may have damaged a rib at best. So he turned the rifle around and opted to use it as a club, just in time, as the skeletal bear was soon upon him.

While Bill held the gun in both hands, the creature sank its jaws into its stock, trying to tear at his face. He had confronted bears before, but nothing quite like this. What death had taken away in bulk, dark magic had returned in aggression, strength and stamina.

Now sensing the softer target of Savannah, who had tripped in the longer grass, the zombie bear spat out the gun and turned to face her. She was some distance from water, the element that gave her power, but thinking quickly from her position on the floor, she could feel the dampness near the spot that had been the skeletal bear's tomb for so long. Stroking the Moonstone necklace, within a few seconds, a large, brown shape rose from the long grass. It then reared like a cobra and struck the monster.

Lucy was disappointed to see that it didn't do much more than cover the beast in a blanket of mud. But that was her sister's intention. For suddenly, she had created a large target for the others, something solid to direct their strikes.

First Brinn attacked with the strimmer-like sticks, then Bill fired two very well directed shots, shattering its pelvis bone and breast plate, important connection points for any bag of bones, living or undead. Soon, as the skeleton started to crumble, Swift was able to shatter the front of the skull with his crutch, which now appeared to have transformed into a trident, or three-pronged spear. The whole bony structure clattered earthward like dozens of boxes of dominoes spilling onto a wooden floor.

As they all looked at each other, flushed and wide-eyed, slowly recovering from the shock, Lucy reached down into the grass.

She re-emerged with what looked like the skeleton of a large mouse or a rat. It had not partaken in the attack and looked, if it was possible for a skeleton to do so, frankly a bit embarrassed.

Swift made as if to smite it, but Bill stayed his arm.

"Ah, look at the poor darling. It's terrified."

Sure enough, when all were silent, they could hear the rattling of the creature's bones, like tiny castanets.

"Well, I am keeping him," Lucy announced, in a voice that would brook no argument. So she popped it on her shoulder and turned to her mother, who was smiling but shaking her head indulgently.

"I don't know for sure what triggered the undead or how, but I do somehow feel that this testing encounter has brought us a step closer to solving the great puzzle of why we are even here."

Bill was still in a state of shock, given what he had seen, so it was left to Swift and Brinn to try to make some sense of the assault.

"It is spoken of, in the legends of our people, that a medicine man used to live on this island, many, many moons before the wood cutters came.

"He was a recluse, a hermit. He lived alone with his carvings. This was before physicians, so, as odd as that may seem, people would come to him for treatment, for very many things that can ail people in this climate. Seemingly he had healing magic, the ways of light to counter the shade."

Brinn nodded, sagely.

"That is not beyond the realms of reasonable," he announced.

Bill, on the other hand, found himself to be the only one who thought the statement strange, given the sights he had just seen.

His mouth was still gaping:

"WHAT?"

"I guess we may have stumbled upon some sort of animal

graveyard, or perhaps the place where he disposed of his food kills.

"Some type of summoning magic could still have been present in the memory of the ancient plants and trees, like the cedar we passed under. The trees always know more than they say.

"Someone may even have set the resurrection magic as a hex or trap intended to keep predatory animals and aggressive tribes at bay."

This time Swift nodded, listening intently.

"If that is true, father, then I very much suspect that, judging by the way your divining rods were behaving, we may just have uncovered a pocket of rare, ancient magic. Some of our people speak of what can happen when our magic users lose their way and their powers become distorted. In the south, Navajo healers have been known to become witches. When the elements align, they adopt animal form, then they are known as skin-walkers."

His handsome face became grave as he spoke.

"We do not like to talk of this dark power, as our magic users heal and use their powers for good. Skin-walker witches are evil, performing twisted ceremonies and manipulating magic in a perversion of the good works medicine people traditionally perform.

"To practice their good works, our traditional healers have to learn about both good and evil, light and shade magic. Most can handle the responsibility, but some people can become corrupt and choose to become witches."

"Indeed," said Elouisa, "indeed …" as if trying to change an uncomfortable subject.

"We all need to stay on our toes, for there is someone else who will doubtless have detected this power too. And she will be a lot more difficult to deal with than a pile of old rodent bones."

As she spoke, the Indian noticed Bill's pale complexion, testimony to his state of shock. So he put his arm around his shoulders.

"I think it's time for you and me to have a proper chat. Did I see you packed beer?" he said, steering the shaken skipper gently across the glade.

What they found across the meadow, surrounded by an impenetrable shield of trees, shed some more light on the mystery.

Wooden carvings stood sentry around what was once a wigwam frame. It had collapsed in on itself and become just a shaded circle in the grass.

Most of the wildlife of the area was captured in the carvings, which Swift explained were probably test pieces for a major project, like a tribal lodge or even a totem pole. Both were objects sacred to the people of origin in these parts.

"See, he would create these individual animals, spirit animals or depictions of our gods as studies, test pieces. He would then, when he was ready and felt he had captured their true essence, turn them into stacked carvings from a single piece of wood, one on top of the other. Last, he would inject holy magic through song and incantation as he carved." He illustrated the steps using a couple of the rotting shapes.

"You have to be a real master to be able to do that from the heart of one tree, without making a single mistake. A slip of a chisel could change the meaning or spell and that would kill the power of the totem by disrespecting the subject."

Lucy's bone rodent was chattering even faster as she bent down to pick up one of the carvings near her foot. As she held it up to the light and pulled off the roots and leaf litter, she could tell that it was the study of a small rabbit.

"Ah!" she said to her new companion. "You? Would this be you?"

The skeletal rodent jumped down onto the sawn-off trunk and stared closely at the subject with its oddly empty eye sockets. Lucy could have sworn that it now looked a little sad, even though it had no muscles or tissues to express feelings. To her, this showed just how complex emotions can be and how subtle the many ways of conveying them.

The others were now finding other familiar creatures crafted in wood. It seemed everything they had just fought was represented in the hermit's work. Seems he had either carved them from trophies or at some point they had all been his companions here in the middle of the woods. Even the mighty bear was carved into the trunk of a dead tree that was still rooted in the soil.

"SHE will have been drawn by the magic in this place," whispered Elouisa to her father, who, judging by his dark mood had been thinking the same thought.

"She must be somewhere not very far from here, unless there is a stronger conductor point where the others are looking."

"I am afraid so. Things have now become very real and unless we find her quickly, she will be nurtured by the power in these ancient ley lines. Her power will grow."

"Yes," replied Elouisa, putting one of the best specimens into her Everbag. "And so close to the primal power of the source of the Firehills, which is clearly raging beyond normal control, she could soon become invincible. Fuelled by that twisted dark magick, she could potentially summon an army of undead to match her spite and her dark ambitions."

Savannah could hear all of this, although it wasn't just the adrenalin from the fight that had her heart beating fast. Swift had taken her hand in his when they both stooped to pick up a carving of a string of leaping salmon cresting a hunting orca cow.

Their eyes met as they raised the statue and despite his caramel-coloured skin, she could still see him blush and then let go, almost dropping the carving on her foot.

He apologised profusely but she simply laughed it off.

Lucy, on the other hand, was onto the moment like a cat on a ball of wool. She now had a huge grin on her face, made all the wider by her sister's obvious discomfort.

And the way the little girl and her new pet giggled conspiratorially made the older girl's blushes bloom.

U p in the tree canopy, Holly and Alice suddenly caught a glimpse of the point they were heading for, the Smoking Mountain. From where they were looking, it was belching mist like a dragon lived within its belly.

"Not that far to go now," Holly shouted to her sister, above the whistling wind, although why she raised her voice she didn't know, given they spoke direct into each other's ears when talking ancient fae.

Looking back to their direction of travel, she was pretty sure she had just seen a dark shape dip beneath the cover of the leaves. But she ignored it for now. To be honest, she had fully expected their crow friend to have made this trip her business too, as their meeting at the den wasn't likely to be a coincidence, entirely.

Down on the ground, James continued to ride the serpent staff while the two young men vied for point as they ran. They had now accepted that their unseen escort was going to be with them the whole way to the mountain, and it was actually quite reassuring.

As they progressed, Bear pointed out strange markings on the trees, arrangements of sticks and ciphers, the symbols of the Coast Salish people.

"They do not normally come this far but these are a sign that they have been camping in this area for some time. There must be a reason."

After a further twenty or so minutes, they arrived at another beach, known locally as Beaver Ho and, sure enough, they could smell and then see a campfire burning.

Various split and staked fish were being slow smoked over the embers and cedar chippings. Oil dripped from the skin and dropped into the fire with a "hiss" that sent up a puff of deliciously scented cedar smoke.

A group of well-toned and burly men wandered over to greet them as they broke from the cover of the trees. They clearly recognised Bear, although were surprised to see two strangers with him, the older of whom was barely breaking a sweat despite the distance he must have just come.

"Greetings, old friend," said the tallest one, who also seemed to be their leader judging by the way the others reacted around him.

"You bring guests," he smiled, his black hair framing his chiselled features and black eyes perfectly. He had an amulet about his neck bearing the sign of a wolf, and a raven's feather in a band in his hair.

Before Bear could answer, the two girls walked into camp looking as fresh as if they had just driven there in an air-conditioned vehicle.

"Ah! And there is a whole tribe of you. We shall have to send the boats out for more fish. And I do not know whether you too have realised, brother, but it is not an easy business being on the water right now."

The full catching up happened over a delicious meal of the tastiest salmon any of them had ever tried. It was served with mashed root of bulrush, which was like potato, and a dipping sauce made from loganberries and juniper blended with wild mint and maple.

The exercise had given them all quite an appetite, especially Henry, who markedly gave the fish a miss yet gorged himself on the rest, supplemented by handfuls of roasted nuts and dried fruit.

"Ah, Henry eats with the ferocity of a grizzly waking from hibernation sleep," laughed the leader who disappointingly was called Red Hand (something to do with a slight birth mark on his face that his people believed signalled he had been touched by the gods).

"It is no surprise that he is your friend," he said, slapping Bear on the shoulder, a little too hard.

"You have very fine children James, I congratulate you. I wish my sons would be so self-assured yet also polite."

Two fine looking lads, the spitting image of their father smiled sheepishly but ventured no comment.

"I am sure their strength is in their modesty," James replied, ever the diplomat.

After the meal, James and Bear took a walk along the shoreline with the chief and his deputy. The latter was a very rare, pale-skinned shaman, or tribal medicine man, an important figure in Indian lore or cultural life.

"We first noticed the problems with the black fish several new moons after the mountains started smoking again.

The logging companies had been cutting some of the ancient stock up near the protected area of the Cougar People. Seems the amount of money they offered finally became too much temptation for someone in that tribe. Honour, it seems, has a price."

James nodded and listened but could see the disappointed in Bear's body language.

"We believe the loggers have ruptured something in the earth near the mountain and this is leeching into the sea and polluting the sound. That is why we have camped here, not just for our festival but to see what we can do to try to restore the balance."

James was relieved by the reality that they had just gained some more important allies, but was disturbed by the implications of what he had just heard.

If the pollutant had been spilling for some weeks, he was concerned whether the impact of the logging activities could have permanently endangered the island's entire orca population.

And if it had affected them so badly, surely it was only a matter of time before it would spread to the rest of the eco-system beneath the sea.

Book 3:

The Totem of Telegraph Bay

She thought about struggling for a second but could see that the claw held her fast and that the Willowand was pinned to her chest.

She could neither work nor call upon magic and to wriggle, to show signs of life, would most likely attract unwelcome attention.

Worst of all, she did not fancy plummeting into the icy waters below, where she could see the fins of the killer whales patrolling.

That evening, the Salish members convinced the group to linger for long enough to witness one of the most sacred rituals of their tribe.

Rehearsals were underway for a great gathering or potlatch, a ceremony in which tribal members give away items as a display of their affluence or success.

They all laughed when Alice said, "So it's a bit like Christmas then?" for there was more than a grain of truth in her innocent wisdom.

As with most social rituals, this ceremony was a way of bonding the community, for coming together, telling stories and sharing traditions that together create a sense of identity, of belonging.

That evening, against a backdrop of the smoking mountain, tribal braves silhouetted by firelight danced what they called the coyote flight. This dance told the story of why there are no coyotes or foxes on the island, their ancestors being driven away by the great cougar king who was envious of their intelligence and distrustful of their cunning.

In their story, they enacted a great battle between the cougar and coyote king, in which the cougar king was poisoned by his treacherous opponent. His tribe were so outraged that they rose up and drove the coyotes into the sea. But while hunting them down they were cursed by the last coyote to leave. His curse was that the cougars would never find their way back to their tribal home again. They would be fated always to be searching but would never find their people or their home. They would become as shadows to each other, powerful apex predators in these parts, but never a community, always alone. This, the legend told, was the reason why the cougars run alone, always searching but never finding their own people.

The guests were enthralled by the storytelling which was all done in the medium of dance and song. Members of the tribe donned ancient robes and animal skins and finely carved masks with exaggerated features. They represented the animals, and a low, rhythmic drumbeat gave the drama a hypnotic quality, as it matched the thumping of their excited hearts.

Cups of herbal tea were handed round, bittersweet but deeply soothing and soon the children had fallen asleep on their father. James gazed lovingly as they snoozed, reflecting on how far they had come together and how grown up they suddenly seemed.

But it wasn't long before he was mesmerised, once more, by the compelling magic in the mystical drama. It reminded him of something Hearne had shown him in Ashridge, before the battle of Berkhamsted.

He spent much of that night in long conversation with their

kind host, gaining more than a glimpse into the future and what he must do next.

They were all awoken at dawn by the chattering of what sounded like a mob of ravens. Then after a swift breakfast, they were soon running with several of the young Salish who had volunteered to miss the festivities to help the higher cause.

After a decent rest, the group was making good time, although James was strangely quiet, discreetly riding the serpent staff once again.

Bear, who was no great talker himself, put this down to the "fire water" he had doubtless shared with their host, plus the inevitable late night. But it was clear to all that the Cornish man had much on his mind.

After about an hour, the mob of ravens burst into another cacophony of noise, so the group increased their pace to get away from them. The Indians were too aware of how these dark birds spoiled many a hunt with their conspiratorial chatter, so their hearts sank at the flight of the black crowd.

The party made the foot of the Smoking Mountain about midday and decided to set up camp while planning their ascent.

They had naturally expected to be joined by their aerial support, the sisters, who were both always eager and helpful around camp. But after ten minutes had passed, alarm bells started to ring.

Several of the men accompanied Henry, who was uncharacteristically agitated at the news and re-traced their trail some way back down their path. But they returned, with no news, no sign, no sighting.

Holly and Alice had seemingly vanished into thin air. Their father's worst nightmare had just manifested itself and he suddenly felt physically ill with worry and fear.

The last thing Alice remembered was taking to the treetops with her sister.

They had flown for a good hour, soaring on the coastal thermals or air currents that dipped and soared in line with the pockets of hot and cold that the trees surrendered to the sky. Then they stopped for a breather, watching a black mob of corvids squabbling in the branches of what looked like a great oak beneath them. They each took several swigs of the cold tea that their hosts had packed for them. Then nothing.

Now they were flying through the air alongside one another again. But this time they were both gagged, bound and each was clasped in the huge talons of what, by the brown and white markings and yellow colouration, not to mention massive, curved and needle-sharp beak, was a bald eagle. But not just any eagle, this one seemed to have the wingspan of an albatross and a torso as large as a Rottweiler dog.

Looking down, Alice could see that they were leaving the Cloud Mountain, their destination, well behind them. They were now heading in the opposite direction and the sound was beneath them, as they could feel the cold from its icy waters against their skin.

Holly was clearly still unconscious, and casting her mind back, Alice remembered her sister being particularly thirsty and drinking twice as much from the buckskin flask.

"Drugged. Treachery!" she spat under her breath. "But why? Surely, they know we're here only to help?" And what of her father and the others? Had their provisions been so spoiled too?

She thought about struggling for a second but could see that the claw held her fast. She also noticed that the Willowand was pinned to her chest.

She could neither work nor call upon magic and to wriggle, to show signs of life, would most likely attract unwelcome attention.

Worst of all, she did not fancy plummeting into the icy waters, where she could see the fins of the killer whales patrolling.

So she had to find a way to control her breathing, to live in the moment and to relax.

By twisting her head round and craning her neck, Holly could see that they were fast approaching the opposite shore. Now her greatest fear became the prospect of being torn apart as lunch in some nursing eagle's tattered nest filled with starving, sharp-beaked chicks.

But the fate in store for the girls was worse than they could even imagine. For the king of the air was flying, not for any nest, mate or family — he was flying to Cougar-Annie's derelict cottage, its bleached boards sighing and groaning in the wind, like sad coffin planks abandoned behind an undertaker's shop.

Worse still, within the cottage that she had just made the centre of her coven, the darkest of necromancers, the occultist at the black heart of this family's tragic back story, lay in wait. And, in the waters of the ancient well, she was watching the progress of her new winged familiar with a sadistic glee.

She knew that these little girls were the key to finally securing unbridled power. She had every idea what her father would do next to save them. And she sensed that her daughter was also very near, a fortuitous happening that would ultimately aid her master plan.

So with the still-warm blood of a dove she had taken from a nest in the willow tree, she wetted a long nail and drew a pentangle on the floor with a foul-practised hand.

Today was working out even better than she could ever have hoped.

Then out of the corner of her eye she caught the reflection of her sharp-toothed smile on a bottle marked poison. She stared until the hate bubbled up and she could no longer suppress a dry, rasping cackle born of tortured morals and a rotting soul.

J ames and Henry were making one last sortie into the forest, searching beneath trees for any sign of the sisters, when they came across two of the wolf pack escort. They had been following the family silently, hoping to have their back should they come under attack, as Long Tooth had suspected they would. But judging by their expressions and the state of their pelts, the news they had was not going to cheer up the humans.

"The crow betrayed us," announced the smaller of the two. "We saw the little ones fall through the canopy about a mile from here. The rest of the escort were with you, but we held back as we had seen the corvids acting strangely. The ravens were behaving like they do when prey is near, which made us suspect something was wrong."

The two wolves moved nearer, and James could see that they were both covered in many small cuts and claw marks, the legacy of a gang attack.

"We tried to get to the girls before anything else, but we were mobbed by the ravens," said the black wolf. "It is very difficult to fight so many, but we have left a dozen or so dead back there. Yet, when we managed to free ourselves, the treacherous crow had taken the little ones, who were not moving, like they were in a deep sleep."

"Henry, warn the others not to drink or eat anything we didn't pack ourselves," snapped James, thinking quickly. Henry set off in were-form, running effortlessly at several times his human pace.

"You have no idea where they have been taken?" asked James, suspecting he already knew the answer.

"Sadly, we do not. When we heard the ravens squabbling, they did say something about returning to "the garden".

"But we do not know what they meant, and we never venture to the other side of these waters because of our truce with the Treekillers."

He seemed embarrassed by the derogatory reference to humans, but James waved his hand to signal that no offence was taken.

"I think you had better warn the alpha pair about what has happened here, and to be wary of the gathering tribes. Seems we need to err on the side of caution, as it is hard to know who to trust right now. Feelings are clearly running high about the grumbling in the mountain that seems to be causing some odd behaviour."

The wolves nodded and made to run back.

"Thank you for what you have done and tried to do for my children. I have no doubt we will meet again, soon."

The two wolves nodded sympathetically, turned and ran back in the direction they had come.

As he watched them go, James reached down and picked up something that had been stuck in the fur of one of them. It was a shiny black flight feather.

And as he stood and stared at it, he found his mind wondering where his girls were now, how frightened they must feel and how helpless he was to save them.

He felt his stomach start to knot and tighten at these thoughts.

Then he too turned and sped back to the rest of their party, working through the fledgling first footings of a plan in his mind.

S tumbling across the studies for the totem would prove to be a much more significant moment for the future of the family and the community than the small party could imagine at the time.

Wiccan ways may differ across continents, but the instincts and sources of power come from the same seam of the mystical. So naturally Elouisa's instincts about the carvings were especially important.

They camped in the glade that evening, after mother had somehow carefully cleansed it of any malevolence. But once they had eaten well, courtesy of Old Bill's kindly wife and lifelong partner, such dreams they all experienced when sleep claimed them.

It was the talk of the campsite the next morning, as the kettle boiled for breakfast and the pan rattled with pancake-making accompanied by the finest maple sauce.

Common to everyone's dreams that night, it seems, was a vision of a frenzied dance at the foot of the mountain. In some, it ended with the earth breaking away and dissolving into the ocean. In another, molten lava descended from above and washed away the revellers. But in Elouisa's version of events, the dancing took place around a large pole, like a macabre English dance in May but by people with many splendid animal masks, worshipping before an arcane statue.

"The totem," announced Swift Hawk, "It is a sacred instrument in the culture of our people. Each object reveals something our tribe respects. We honour our ancestors, our legends and the creatures we rely upon for our way of life in this way. Our finest craftsmen make them. And the best of our craftsmen finds the magic in the wood and blend it with the magic in the objects they carve to create power for the community."

They were all enraptured by his explanation.

"They are no mere decoration. They are spirits and each totem pole brings a special power all of its own."

"Just by carving?" asked Lucy innocently.

"Much depends on the skill of the one carving and what he is creating, little one. What we saw yesterday? That is a sign that the ancient one who lived here and carved those animals was a shaman of great power."

"A medicine man?" asked Savannah.

The Indian looked into her eyes as he replied.

"That is the word your people often use. But to us, the shaman is second only to the chief. He is a respected elder and has great power, handed down his family line and captured in his work."

They all went silent at this point, deep in thought and reflecting on what they had faced the day before.

Brinn was the first to break the mood.

"We, of course, have people who fulfil similar roles in our culture. Although most people rarely see them anymore, so obsessed have we become with material, man-made things. The mystical world is never far away from the surface of what surrounds us."

"Indeed," said Elouisa. "This isn't getting us much closer to finding out what we're here to discover, now is it?"

"So, where next, skipper?"

Bill was wide eyed but exhilarated by what he had seen and heard the last few days and although shocked, the twinkle in his eyes and encouraging smile gave the impression he was having the time of his life.

"I dread to say, but it's either a hack through the dense undergrowth inland or…"

"We return to the boat and risk running the gauntlet of the orcas again?" enquired Brinn.

"Well…that's one way of putting it but, yes."

"The boat it is then," said Elouisa, leading the way before the debate lengthened. "Better the finned devil you know, eh?"

As they started to make their way back across the glade, when they ducked under the bridge tree, Lucy noticed something glinting in the early morning sun.

Reaching down and picking it up, she brushed off some persistent mud and saw it was some sort of marble made of black stone. Nobody had noticed as she was at the back, so she licked it and gave it a polish. Then with the taste of red earth in her mouth, she paused to examine it closely as it had a familiarity about it.

The orb felt warmer than she expected, but she shrugged, smiled and popped it in her pocket, hoping she had just got away with a rare secret moment before her mother looked back to see where she was.

Patting her pocket, she jogged a little to tag onto the back of the line heading back to the unpredictable sound and whatever the sadly disturbed sea creatures had in store for them.

"Cougar-Annie's place is the next bay round," shouted Bill, above what was quite a fierce wind now whipping round the sound.

"We'll be heading into this gale, so will take a might longer than expected, but we'll be fine," he announced.

"He's tempting fate with those famous last words," thought Brinn, and sure enough, no sooner had the thought left his head than they spotted something falling from the sky.

"Heads down," shouted their Indian companion, as a large log came crashing onto the top deck, missing Brinn by a whisker.

"Get down below," cried the captain as, on the horizon, three or four eagles were gliding in on the wind, clutching at more objects which they then launched into the slipstream like missiles.

The next, a sizeable rock, came in at face height and smashed into the instrument deck, taking out the radio.

"Agh," shouted Bill, as shards of glass from broken instruments cut his cheek. "They're coming again, I need to switch controls," and with that, he slammed the boat into cruise mode, nose to the current for stability, and made for the metal stairway. He wasn't fast enough, however, and another piece of wood caught him in the square of the back, knocking him into the rail and winding him.

Had Swift not been at hand, the next blow could well have finished the elderly man. But the warrior made a shield from a fold out tabletop and used this to cover him while he scooped Bill into a fireman's lift and carried him down the stairs.

In the meantime, Brinn had remained on the top deck and was battling, not with the boat but with the wind. As a Druid, his greatest power comes from nature and while he couldn't mind-merge with the birds attacking them, for reasons unknown, he could influence the natural conditions somewhat.

So Brinn diverted half the wind, bent it and created a spinning vortex which he used to catch the raptors and send them into the tree canopy, flailing head over claw.

With his other hand, he directed the rest of the Easterly wind to buffer the boat from the central current where it had drifted, back to the shore, while Elouisa took to the controls, spinning the wheel and adjusting the throttle to battle the water.

Just as this partnership seemed to have saved the day, their worst fears were realised and Lucy, from a deck down, spotted three black sail-like dorsal fins heading straight for them.

"The killer whales!" she shouted above the gale.

But before she could look round, both her sister and Swift Hawk had taken to the treacherous water.

Elouisa continued to point the boat toward the target bay,

oblivious to Lucy's warning. Brinn was preoccupied with his work and Bill was still writhing in pain. So, the youngest Savage did what the bravest would do and that was the best she could think of. She rubbed the Ravenring, not to release anything, but to unleash its other major power, the mind-meld with animals she had last used in the battle at Berkhamsted castle.

What Lucy had not bargained for, was that she was attempting to meld with minds that were disturbed and, it seems very, very angry.

Suddenly she was virtually under the water, seeing everything from the perspective of the dominant bull whale. And he was raging, his mind a ball of misery. Raging at what the people had done to his family; raging at the poisons in the water and, right now, raging at the two half-fish who were between him, his brothers and the blue-hulled boat.

Lucy was shocked to see her sister, visible before her in absolute technicolour under water. Yet she looked so small and delicate, compared to those behemoths of the deep.

Lucy concentrated on convincing the bull orca that she was no risk, that she was kind, one of them. Savannah only wanted peace, to understand what was wrong. She could now sense doubt in the bull's mind, for he was slowing, pausing, signalling to the others that he was calling off the charge, the attack. She could see that they had slowed down too and rather than heading straight for Savannah, they swam on past her and made to turn.

A soothing feeling of relief swept over Lucy. But she maintained her meld, her connection with the magnificent sea creature.

Then, however, her heart leaped into her mouth as she realised that something was wrong. Where was Savannah's companion? Where had…?

Then she felt the pain as suddenly as the orca did. The three-pronged trident piercing his side.

"No!" she found herself thinking and shouting.

But the connection had been severed by the agony. As readily as turning off a light switch.

Rushing to the side of the boat, the worst of her fears were confirmed. All three sets of dorsal fins had now turned, and all were heading at pace back towards where her sister could just be seen, her glorious aura glinting under the clear water.

"No!" Lucy screamed in terror.

Then she did the only thing left to her. She did something on impulse. Without thinking twice, Lucy climbed up onto the rail and threw herself into the fast-rushing water. She hurled her tiny fragile body, right into the path of the angry killer whales.

Henry was concerned about his father's state of mind. For once it wasn't the other way round. James was always the one everyone looked to for calm. He was their anchor. But the capture of the girls was hurting him many times more than if he had been attacked directly. He was visibly in pain. And the worst blow was from the weapon of not knowing, not being able to predict who had taken them and what their intentions were.

Their group contained no seers and although he was a powerful warlock, James did not have the gift of second sight. So, he turned his inner vision onto solving that problem as a priority, a problem that also implied revenge.

First, he interrogated the men who were running with them. The telling spell he employed was incredibly strong and it became clear, quite quickly, that they were not party to the treachery. This came as a relief as it probably meant not all the Coast Salish were involved.

They left the Indians at the mountain to keep watch, then Henry and James circled back and double-timed the pace, making it in half the time.

James barely paused for breath as they reached the busy beach again, slipped from the staff and continued marching forward while raising the weapon in his sword arm in one fluid movement.

The elders looked surprised but pleased to see them as he expected. All except for the shaman. He took one look at Henry in were-form and turned and fled towards the deep wood. But when he got there, four snarling wolves were waiting.

"Aaaaa! No! Please, please, I beg you!" he screamed.

But as he turned again, Henry hit him in his stomach and dropped him to the beach, the man suddenly feeling his hot breath and running saliva.

"What is the meaning of this, James?"

The chief was now walking over to the fallen medicine man, wary of Henry's mood and the proximity of the wolves.

"She made me do it. Mother of crows. The cougar mistress. She came to me in the flames, offering salvation for the sacrifice of just two of them.

"She wanted the changeling sisters, that is all. She said they were the reason why the smoke has come to the mountain and in delivering their souls, she would end the spell of harming."

Red Hand, the tribal chief, said that he could not believe what he was hearing. And with a wave of his arm, he commanded that the shaman be taken away.

"Wait a minute," said James. Let me have a word with him."

He crouched down to the prone man's level.

"Do you have the gift of second sight?"

"Yes, I can have."

"Well then you are going to find my girls and you are going to find them now, or you are no use to me and I WILL feed you to the wolves."

The man nodded frantically, terror in his eyes.

"I will need an eagle's feather and something from you or your child."

"Will this do?" growled Henry, as he picked up the man's hand and licked it with his long, rough tongue, accidentally grazing his palm with one of his incisors as he did, drawing a line of blood.

James was already walking towards the fire, the tribal members going silent out of respect as he passed them.

It took the shaman a few minutes to make the seeing cipher, using the feather which he rubbed between the palms of his hands, then dipped it into the blue flames and inhaled the smoke it gave off.

They saw his eyes roll to the back of his skull and turn white as he collapsed to his knees. Then he started speaking in tongues, a garbled array of sounds coming from his open mouth.

Bear sat down next to James and started translating.

"He is saying that he is the eagle lord and he has taken the spirits in human form that were gathered by the corvids, the crow and the raven.

"He is flying with them, as commanded, a prize for his mistress in the home of the cougar's sorrow. This is the place where the insects gather. This is now the sorceress' home."

With this the shaman gasped, his pupils rolled back into view and he plunged his head into his open hands.

James sat for a few seconds more, to make sure he had exhausted every measure of intelligence as well as translate it. Then he turned to Bear and the chief and shrugged. "Do you know the place he was referring to, where the eagle has taken them?"

"There is only one place it can be, and it is back across the water, James," said Bear. "It must be the place they call Cougar-Annie's garden. But, sorry, the sorceress he refers to means nothing to me."

James was staring at the shaman as he came round, clearly still frightened.

Two warriors closed in on him, but James signalled for them to stand their ground.

"Despite what he has done," said James to Red Hand, "I have a sense that we are going to need to use him again before all of this is over. And he is the only connection we have with the girls right now. So, against all our better judgement, let's go easy on him."

"How much more of that sleeping poison did you make?" demanded the chief.

The shaman handed over a small shell flask.

"Drink it!"

"But I…" he could see that it was futile to argue, so reluctantly he tipped it into his mouth.

"All of it…"

So, he upended the container again and drained the last drop.

Then he closed his eyes.

Soon, the traitor slumped onto his side, hitting the ground with a dampened thud.

Savannah saw the shape descending through the water out of her peripheral vision, because merfolk see through water like the rest of us see through air.

Without a second's thought for her own safety, despite the onrushing orcas, she swam straight for her sister, who was about ten feet beneath the sea caught by a rip current.

But even faster to react was Hawk, who with a flick of his muscular tail headed straight for her, arriving just as the bull whale opened his huge jaws.

What the merman did next defied belief.

He swam straight into the orca's mouth and jammed his spear behind its upper teeth.

Savannah was so shocked by his action that she hesitated for a second. But that was enough for one of the other onrushing bulls to take Lucy in its mouth. Then, to her horror, it swam off with her, riding the current.

"NO!" Savannah screamed in panic, giving chase. The orca was fast, especially with the current at its back, but she was frantic and charged with adrenalin. Strangely the whale appeared to lurch to the natural slipway on the island they had just left and was now spy-hopping, poking most of its upper body out of the water. Then, with one flick of its fluke, or huge tail, it part-beached itself.

In an obvious state of understandable distress, Savannah swam right up behind the whale and then surfed up its back and onto its head.

She was screaming panicked commands in his language, "Do not harm her."

However, what she saw when she got there was not what she was expecting.

Her sister, although belching salt water, appeared to be fine and was lying on the sand. The whale, meanwhile, was nudging her delicately away from the water.

"Oh!" was all that came to Savannah's mind. Then she felt guilty for mounting the great beast in such rough fashion, especially when it asked, quite politely, "Do you mind jumping down, pretty mermaid? You are standing on my blow hole."

As she slid down the side of her unwitting host, she was greeted with the sight of Hawk flying unceremoniously through the air.

The giant bull had clearly had enough of his dental work and had tossed him from his mouth, onto the rocky beach.

Savannah called over to him as she knelt by Lucy.

"Are you ok?"

The look he gave her was one of embarrassment, tinged with disbelief and not a little relief.

"I'll live," he said sulkily. "Seems the worst of the bruising is to my ego."

The orca with Lucy was clearly very concerned, but enjoying the attention she was lavishing on him as she stroked his beak.

The other two were now spy-hopping and seemed to be sharing a joke about "nasty tasting fish, but worse dental skills".

"Luckily, Hawk can't hear them," Savannah thought.

Back on the boat, somehow Elouisa and Brinn had managed to steer into the bay they had intended to travel to and were securing the lines. The extent of the drama they had just been party to had clearly yet to become apparent to them.

Old Bill was helping by shouting instructions.

With everyone more or less safe and accounted for, Savannah decided it was high time they got some answers.

So, leaving her sister to charm her latest friend, far too large to be called a pet, she slid back into the water and to the amazement of her fondest admirer, she swam back out to the two gigantic blackfish.

Back aboard the Okwaho, where they would now rest and recover from their latest ordeal, Brinn and Elouisa rustled up some mugs of warm, sugary tea and chocolate cookies for the shock.

"So, you're telling me that these whales are blaming the pollution from the fishing boats and the logging for the dwindling fish stocks and THAT is why they have taken over the sound?" said Bill, as Savannah relayed the conversation.

"Well, that's what they have just told me. That and the mysterious illness that has befallen too many of them now. I told you about the ones I found with the canker-like growth around their blow holes? Well apparently, that has only started happening since promises were broken and the logging started in the sacred ground by the mountain."

"So, they are mad at the loggers and have been trying to get a message to all humans by shutting down the ports," added Hawk, who was still nursing a bruised bum; given mermen may be able to glide, but are not so great at landing on rocky beaches it seems.

"Had you not been here, we may never have found out the reason. But I'm pretty sure the state authorities will look to clear the sound by force unless this comes to an end soon, or we can convince them otherwise.

Personally, I'm not so sure how we just say that we know coz our mermaid spoke to 'em." Bill rightly looked concerned as he moved gingerly about the deck.

"Well," said Brinn, "the goddess cave sent us here through the portal for a reason.

"Now it is becoming clearer what that reason is and it seems many lives and livelihoods depend on us doing the right thing, whatever that may be."

"Yes, Father," interjected Elouisa, "that may be so. But we are all forgetting one other factor."

All eyes turned to Brinn. The colour drained from his face as he replied.

"No. I, of all people, have certainly not forgotten that one of the main reasons we are here is to counteract whatever dark and miserable plan has been brewing in the mind of the sea wytch."

"Ah! Mother!" Elouisa muttered. "Just when we thought we were making progress, we're right back at Mother again."

When the shaman awoke, they were at the foot of the Smoking Mountain. Red Hand had sent extra men to make sure he did as he was bidden.

"So, you're back!" exclaimed Henry, back in human guise. James was in a conversation circle with the others and looked up at this news.

He wandered over.

"Against my better judgement, I am going to trust you. Because I believe you love this place as well, it being your home and you want no more harm to come to the land or sea."

His captive nodded, slowly.

"Well we need you, as a respected elder, to speak with the elders of the tribe on the land under the mountain. We need you to convince them that the ancient tree killing is wrong, and that it is causing chemicals to spill from the lava on the mountain into the ocean and it must stop.

"Do you think you can try?"

He nodded his agreement and so they set off on the final leg, looking for the mountain tribe.

They had not gone very far when shadows appeared before them. One minute there was an open trail. The next, there stood two aloof warriors.

They wore full buckskin tunics, such was the colder air here, and the mark they bore was of the great blackfish, or the orca.

"Greetings, friends. What brings you to the Great Whale Mountain land?"

The shaman stepped forward and quickly relayed the nature of their mission.

He clearly did justice to the story, for they were shortly following the warriors up the hill to the first plateau where the tribal settlement currently sat.

It was a hive of activity, as they appeared to be breaking camp.

The chief, a man of a great many seasons marked out in his fine silver mane, came forward to greet their visitors.

"Apologies for a distracted greeting, friends," he said warmly. "We are preparing for a move to different ground, as you can see. For the god mountain has scorched much of the earth above us, for the sins of others."

He took them into the grandest of the remaining shelters, where they exchanged news and both parties were brought up to speed.

The chief, aptly but rather poetically named Sunlance, nodded in a dignified way throughout, as if he were hearing news he was expecting.

"We did not believe that the tree killers would harvest so much of the ancient wood as they have. I am afraid to say that my people became blind with greed.

"The crow came to us with a powerful vision of the offer we would receive and how we would become a great tribe with our riches.

"Then the wood companies came with offers of much money. So, some wished to settle in the new houses and were bewitched by the offers of riches.

"But now we are all paying the price, as the spirts are angered. The mountain spits poison, releases angry fumes and burns the things we love.

"We have no choice now but to move from our ancestral places."

"You saw the great crow too?" said James, taking the bowl of berries offered.

"The trickster? Yes. We have seen her many times in the history of our tribe. That one is known to us and was known to our ancestors. But she has vanished since the troubles started."

Henry was listening to the discussion and watching the tribal members readying themselves for the move. They dismantled the beautifully painted and embroidered tents with great skill.

Everything seemed to have a place and there was a place for everything.

A group of what appeared to be elders were supervising the removal of some of the more sacred artefacts, judging by the care taken. These included several of what Henry recognised from his own studies as tribal shields and totem poles.

At the centre of them all was a mighty, ornately carved and well-weathered pole that was well over twenty feet tall, and to which the men were paying particular attention, despite the fact it appeared to be charred and burnt at the top.

"I see you admiring our prime tribal totem, young brave."

The chief had wandered over to Henry now.

"That was once the focus for all our power, the gateway between our people now and our ancestors who we celebrate in our dances and our stories and our songs. When we lived on our village on stilts, in what is now known as Telegraph Bay, that we called Blackfish Water, that was on the outskirts of our land. It controlled the fish, brought great abundance and protected us from harm, it was a signal to the animals that we respected them, but had dominion over them. It was an ancient pact with them."

"It's, it's amazing. But …but why is it burned so?"

"Well, that moment of burning marked the moment the troubles came, and our time of sadness fell like storm clouds.

"The spirts came down upon our tribe from the Black Fish mountain here in a bolt of sky fire and they struck the gateway key. It was a sign that our control over the animals was gone. And so, you have seen, they no longer respect us because of our greed."

As they talked, they were walking closer to the totem, which was carefully being lowered using only ropes, sweat and muscle.

Henry could gradually see one carving slip into view atop another, as if the creatures were standing on each other's shoulders in an eternal struggle for dominance. It reminded him of his own internal torment as if it reflected how he felt at times, balancing boy and beast.

A large black crow propped up the base of the totem; wings spread and beak jutting defiantly, then a snarling, indomitable bear. Both were carved in obsidian black with red and white outline in the distinctive style of the peoples of the region.

In the midst of the bestial wrestling match, the artist had carved two people. They had blank expressions, as if stripped of emotion. But unmistakable war paint anointed their warrior faces and crude tribal weapons, sinew and willow bows and stone axes were in their hands.

Immediately above them swam a mighty blackfish orca, pursuing a leaping salmon. It was both graceful and powerful, magnificent despite having the face of a bizarre demon carved into its belly.

But, try as he might, Henry couldn't quite make out what was at the top. It may or may not have been riding the great black fish. It seemed to have a muscular human body and a shape implying four active limbs and was covered in strange ridges and had what looked like fangs…"

"I see you are drawn to the apex, the pinnacle, our totem spear point." He could see that Henry was staring at the tip of the pole.

"Well, that was what the spirits damaged most when the problems last came, and they first sent down their great lance of fire."

He gestured with his hand.

"For depicted there, wrought by our master necromancer carver on a night filled with spirit magic, there astride the mighty black fish, he captured the essence of the great manwolf.

"There you see our chief land god. He is lord of the mountains and all who reside upon them.

"It is He who has kept order here for many, many generations. "It is He who spews fertility, who makes things thrive and grow.

"But now, it is He who was taken, who has gone. He let the malign spirits in and brought the age of darkness and wild chaos upon us.

"So, my ancient people weep as the mountains weep. Our minds are confused as the mountain is clouded and the water, it becomes heavy and salty with our too-many tears."

At first sight, Cougar-Annie's garden is a triumph of nurture over nature, the will of people over the weight of what has always been.

With little more than her own two hands, this first-footing pioneer turned a wilderness into a cultivated land, a green oasis into a riot of colour and a desolate outpost into a business that just about sustained a family.

She infamously fought a battle with the wildlife using traps, alarms and firearms that made the bravest of predators think twice before trespassing. Yet despite carving out a brutal existence for her long-suffering family, she ultimately lost the war, and her post was abandoned when this legendary pioneering lady finally became part of the very ground she had fought to tame.

So, it was with mixed feelings that, in the lands that Annie once roamed, the now battle-hardened party returned to the trail. Their destination was Cougar-Annie's homestead, her domain and they were rightly nervous about what they would find. For, as they would soon discover for themselves, there was truth in the tales that while she was long dead and in the ground, her spiritual essence lingered long.

The party hadn't long been trekking when they detected small signs of human habitation, rusted relics of a bygone age. The very mooring posts reeked of a time when it would have taken a grown man an hour of his life to saw through such a stump.

Flotsam and jetsam scattered about the beach told tales of previous visitors as rusted metal and sea-polished glass blended with pebbles and faded wooden signs spoke a half-language forgotten for good.

They wound their way through what were clearly foreign flowering bulbs, trees and shrubs that seemed oddly out of place with the hardier native species. Forests of rhododendrons thrived here and there but were still strangers to the natural stock as if reluctantly blooming side by side with Canadian evergreens, like strangers in unseasonal clothing. Hawk in particular was taken by their shapes and forms and colours, especially the yellow of daffodils and tulips which he had not seen anywhere else on Vancouver Island.

As children, his people were warned off coming here, as if the force field of spiteful hostility left by the hard-nosed founding mother of this place still exerted its power. His people were all about balance and symbiosis, flowing with nature. She was all about subduing it, bending it to her needs and will.

Winding through what must once have been vegetable beds judging by the way they sat upon rather than in the landscape, unlike the mosses, lichens and ferns that seemed to enfold it, they stumbled across an ancient fruit tree. It was inevitably gnarled by the many tests and trials of the weather. Yet it had still not been accepted as a native as nothing else grew near. The tree reminded Brinn of the wise apple that grew on the coastal path near Coverack, adders and garlic at its roots.

"Pear," said Brinn, "and apple over there," he pointed with his staff.

"Not quite ripe, which is a shame. But this must have been the genesis of an orchard at one point."

"Blessed are the people who have the foresight to plant trees. For under their shade, they are unlikely to rest for long, if at all."

"What on earth is this?" Lucy had stepped into one of the large clumps of grass, attracted by a very ramshackle structure of sorts, that could possibly have once been an out-house but was most likely home to mini-beasts feasting on the decay.

She was tugging on a very old board of some kind.

Savannah grabbed a corner and gave her a hand to pull it clear of the creepers, roots and weeds.

"Well," said Old Bill curiously, "That about looks like the remains of a case for what, in the olden days, we used to call stuffed things."

Lucy was picking up a collection of white, ridged discs and examining them.

"Now I'd be guessin' what you have there, young Lucy, is bones."

She dropped the discs as her reflex action kicked in.

"Yup, there's some broken glass panes over there. I'm guessin' that was once a pile of leather 'n' fur, 'n' sawdust, 'n'…."

"Teeth?" offered Hawk, holding up what was clearly the jawbone of a predator, given the prevalent incisors or fangs.

"Yup! Cougar teeth at that, I'd say. And given Annie's reputation, I'd wager, if you stick around here long enough, there's every chance you'd uncover dozens more skeletons like this one. Now, given what we encountered back in that glade…."

Then he suddenly turned off the tap of his enthusiasm, recalling the full horror of what happened the day before. But just as he did, a blood curdling scream ripped through the air.

It was Hawk.

He had taken a couple of extra steps into the high clump of grass, hoping to find the other half of the head when something like burning jaws of fire had clasped his left leg, dropping him dramatically to the floor.

"Aaagggghhh!" he cried, rocking back and forth in agony. "Get it off me!"

Surprisingly deftly for a man of his years, Brinn was the first into action. He pulled his hand scythe from his cloak and carefully cut back the brush around the fallen warrior. But it soon became obvious what had befallen him.

"A man-trap," he grimaced. "And by the looks of it, rusted badly."

"A trap for men?" asked Lucy, innocently.

"Not for, but by. Sorta thing Cougar-Annie woulda used to catch cougars n bears n such," said Bill.

He was already working at the release mechanism with a stout stick, but the rust wasn't helping resolve matters.

"Please, let me take a look," said Elouisa, conscious of how their companion's pain was impacting the group.

Hawk was now quite pale, from the pain of the jaws biting into the bone of his lower leg.

She took out her dagger, which made the Indian shy away a little, but after looking into her eyes, he relaxed again.

Studying the jaws of the trap for a few seconds, she aimed the blade at a particular part of the mechanism and then, with a single blow from the Jade Athame, she cut through the spring loading. With a hiss, the jaws snapped open.

"Ohhh!" their victim cried, with obvious relief.

"The trouble is far from over, as the risk of infection and even blood poisoning is very high. I need everyone to look for herbs and grasses that should grow close by. But whatever you do, do not put your feet where your eyes don't go first."

With that, she reeled off a list of her requirements including bark of willow and rosemary and set them all on their way. In the meantime, she fetched salt water from the sea and the first aid chest from the boat. She rustled around in it for a bit then pulled out an aerosol can with a triumphal look.

"Really? You?" joked the warrior, clearly feeling slightly better as he had time for humour.

"Well, not everything about the modern world is worse than every aspect of the old ways."

As she said this, distracting him, she cleaned the wound carefully and applied the antiseptic spray.

The Indian winced at how it smarted on the open wound.

"But worry not," she whispered jokingly, "my witch doctor poultice will be applied just as soon as my band of minions ticks everything off my shopping list."

Even the badly injured Hawk had to laugh at the notion of Old Bill posing as a witch's familiar.

Overhead, un-noticed, silhouetted against the bright sky, a great bald eagle circled, blotting out the sun for a second and then for him, all went dark as well.

The wytch treated the brave young man's wounded leg with the first aid kit and a soothing spell. But Elouisa was soon looking down upon an unconscious man, as the ancient magic took hold. She allowed herself a moment with her thoughts and surveyed the wilderness in silence as the patient slept. She could understand why a woman would want to live alone here aligned with and pitted against the elements, especially given the harsh realities of town living at the time. She imagined the triumph of planting and harvesting your own food, of watching a family survive hand to mouth on nature's bounty and that took her mind back to those days in Ashridge with Henry and Alice and simpler times. She smiled. But the black dog of her depression was never far off and as a cloud drifts before the sun, reality soon slunk around the corner once more, casting a cold shadow over her unconscious mind.

"This is usually a sign of the pull of the dark magick", she thought to herself, worried. Talking to herself like this was a technique she used for coping; to acknowledge rather than consume the problem and then work consciously to resist the dark force within.

"This inner cold must mean that SHE is somewhere close now," Elouisa muttered, inadvertently placing a hand on the Jade Athame and pulling up her hood for comfort. "She'll never give up until…"

Something rustled in the shrubs a couple of feet away. And then again. But before she could investigate, the girls returned with more of the medicinal herbs. They were followed by the men, carrying a large rock with a shallow basin, perfect for grinding and pounding with a round stone.

"Nice work," she said, genuinely impressed. "We'll make a Wiccan of you yet, Captain Bill," she joked, just to watch his discomfort.

"Um, well, I've seen enough weird to say that I'm just fine with my knife 'n' gun. There's an honesty in the Canadian colonial version of the old-fashioned ways."

Brinn laughed. "Nothing more old-fashioned than these ancient arts," he said, "here in Canada too" while his daughter slowly waved her palms over the bunch of cut flowers and weeds, muttering an incantation under her breath before starting the pounding.

The two men, bonded by breadth of experience, took a walk toward another group of trees, while the girls watched and soaked up their mother's ancient art.

As they got closer, their small talk was interrupted when they noticed a huge crow sitting on one of the lower boughs of another ancient apple tree. It watched them closely with its black bead eyes.

"My, that's a fine big specimen," said Bill. "Almost eagle size. Do a lotta damage with that bone-crusher up front," he said, talking about the black beak.

As if to answer him, the bird let out a couple of the strange squawk-like cries, so parrot-like, the corvid sounds that characterise the breed.

"Sadly that is often the last sight too many baby lambs see before these death-bringers work their mischief. I was once a farmer and take it from me, they're brutal."

"They are only enacting where the chain of life has placed them, Bill," said Brinn, in a resigned tone. He then cupped his hand over his mouth and replied to the bird in kind.

The crow tilted its head one way, then the other, as if listening. It was hypnotic, engaging, drawing them closer to stare into the dark marble pools that were its eyes. And then, with no warning whatsoever, Brinn was taken in the ribs by a massive cougar, that barely made a sound until it had him in its teeth.

The air was instantly thick with cries of beast and man. Fortunately, despite his advanced years, Bill had not lost his reflex speed and while the druid grappled with the predator on the ground, he swiftly flipped his rifle from his shoulder.

It was too risky to shoot into the mass of cloth, fur and wrestling flesh. So, to the cacophony of the crows cawing in his ears, he swung the butt of the rifle in an arc and with a skilfully aimed blow, smashed the beast across the muzzle. He could feel it impact with the lion's incisor teeth.

The cougar, which had an incredibly square face and fearsome look, screamed, rolled and was blinking with the pain, but held fast. It was accustomed to absorbing blows from the hooves of prey animals. It wasn't letting dinner go without a battle. So Bill struck again and again until, with a roar like a racing car exhaust, it let Brinn go and turned to face its tormentor.

The new combatant pairing circled to the right, each examining the other waiting, probing for an opening. So Lucy did the first thing she could think of upon returning, having heard the noise. She picked up and threw her Indian friend's abandoned spear in the direction of his assailant. She wasn't adept at using it, so it simply landed in front of the cat, however. As if insulted, the beast now turned its attention to the comparatively softer and smaller target.

Snarling, the cougar charged toward the smallest girl and her mother, who was still on her knees tending to Hawk.

Savannah, who also ran back, panting, found herself lost for a water source close enough to do much. She just screamed.

This did at first confuse but then it enraged the animal further. It made a split-second decision and soon resumed flying through the air toward Lucy.

She was pressing the Ravenring desperately at this point. But to no avail. Something about the proximity of the crow was causing interference. Meanwhile her tiny skeletal familiar clacked its jaws in panic, running around her shoulders like a boy on a burning deck.

"Something is blocking it," she shrieked.

"My ring won't work. Help me, it's going to eat me Mummy!"

Abandoning her charge and acting on a mother's instinct, Elouisa reached for her dagger and sprang in front of her daughter. Her modest weapon was now glowing like her fear and anger. The cat would be upon them in a heartbeat now. But before anyone could do anything else an ear-splitting thunderclap tore the air.

With that the great cat fell at her feet, like a sack, stone dead.

"Are you ok?" said Bill, a few seconds later, rifle in one hand and the older man's robe in the other.

"I don't believe it did much damage, although it has shaken me up," said Brinn, pulling out the sickle kept inside his robes which seemingly had absorbed most of the killer bite.

"Surprised it didn't break its teeth."

Despite their ordeal, Lucy was now kneeling by the magnificent cougar.

There was no celebration. She was actually crying.

"Why? Why did it have to go for us?"

"That is just the way nature works, Lucy," her sister said, arm round her shoulder. "It was just doing what it always has."

But as she uttered the words, Bill and Brinn looked at each other, knowing that it was very unlike an animal known for stealth to attack in the middle of the day and to go for fully grown adults in a group.

Something about this was very wrong. It felt like some sort of sacrifice, like a distraction and Brinn couldn't help but think that the person they now sought had an awful lot to do with what had just taken place.

Incredibly, nobody seemed that much the worse for wear. The ruckus had managed to wake Hawk as Elouisa was tying off the bandage she had applied to his leg.

"Steady," she said, as he shivered and tried to get to his feet, sensing that this was no time to be napping.

"Just take it a bit easy for a few seconds for the magic to work. Here, drink some of this." She handed him a flask of apparently restorative potion, which surprisingly tasted agreeable, judging by his expression.

"Not bad for cobra gall bladder and rhino urine for strength, eh?" she joked, just to see his mouth turn south.

She then let Savannah take over and wandered over to Brinn.

"Judging by the way the Moonstone is glowing around your eldest granddaughter's neck, I would say the object of our inevitable attention is remarkably close, wouldn't you?"

"Oh, no doubt about that. The cat was completely melded and beyond my control, and I know she is going to have other delights planned. How these thoughts take me back...and not in a good way."

"The plan was to locate her, not to tackle her," interjected his daughter. "We need all of us for that, and to understand the source of the power that has drawn her here."

"And we should stick to that plan. But we must presume she is wise to us now. Her spies, like that crow, will have informed her of our number. So, if we explore more now, we have to do it with much caution."

Elouisa looked doubtful, feeling a throbbing in her head and a sinking sensation in the pit of her stomach.

She had taken the large black book titled **The Legend of the Lost** from her Everbag and had been studying the spell pages intently, as she sometimes did when needing to focus. The book famously guides the reader to the passages it feels they most need, much like a search engine on a computer. But now the writing seemed somehow clearer and crisper, and her attention drawn compellingly to certain pages over others. This was presumably because the artefact was closer to the one who penned much of its content than it had been for a long time.

Elouisa couldn't help but wonder too, whether the mysteries of the book would stay true to her or be permanently wedded to the alpha wytch. Artefact loyalty is a tricky non-science. They can never be truly trusted as they are fallible, like the best people. But she made and memorised her selections, regardless. Then she looked up and answered the question her father left hanging in the air.

"Well, we don't exactly have much choice but to finish what we started here. The destruction she will cause across this continent will dwarf what she did back at our home, at the castle or the unnatural events in Cornwall if we do not confront her.

"But we were hardly a match for her before, what makes you so sure now?"

He could only look on as she spoke.

"I have felt her claws at my gut now for a lifetime. Her grip on me has been getting worse from the moment we landed."

Brinn was now seated on a low tree stump and gazed up at her with his deep, dark, unblinking eyes, full of concern, love and not a little pity.

"Remember, she carries the weight of generations of bitterness," he counselled. "It focuses but also blinds her."

"It will be eating away at her, weakening her. But we have the combined power and perspective of all of us and the sacred artefacts that chose us, that channel our strength.

"Her power comes from forcing and controlling things. Ours comes to us, willingly, attracted by goodness. There is a vital difference."

Elouisa was scanning the long grass as he spoke. She knew he was trying to comfort her. But it wasn't working all that well.

"She has always managed to bring her will to bear and half of us are missing, Father. I miss James. He is always so certain and unmoving. And the children bring…a completion to our puzzle, a balance that you must feel as well. She has always made me feel, inadequate, lost, blinded, like she retains pieces of my soul."

At this he first looked pained but the gaze softened into a smile.

"You have been strengthened, not weakened by her coercive manipulation, daughter. The years that were stolen from you by alienating the children have made you resilient and wise. Have faith. We will be reunited again. They won't be long. We have enough power and will to hold her. And once unified there is no force that can tear us apart again."

He smiled and took her hands, eyes sparkling with deep

kindness. "I have a feeling the pattern will be completed soon. All the pieces will be in place."

As they spoke, he had been quietly arranging beach pebbles. He had placed them almost absentmindedly, one on top of the other, balanced precariously.

"You must trust in James. Believe in our line. Be inspired by the light. But break from her control. The darkness has taken too strong a hold there. She will never return now.

"We may sometimes be apart, but with a clean conscience the good in you is never really lost. And even she knows that."

With this he reached down, picked something up and then stood to hug her.

It was a long, from the toes up hug. It was much needed. And when it was over, he pressed something into her hand as he wandered back to see how their friend was healing.

She looked down at the object in her palm.

It was something so simple and yet it instantly meant such a lot.

It was a heart fused from the pebbles he had been arranging.

However, despite being made from stone, it wasn't cold at all. In fact, it was blood-warm to her touch.

Book 4:

The Changeling Returns

"He is the love that dare not speak its name.

He is Goddess Teote's eternal shame.

He is the child that should not have been.

He must not be once again.

He must be sacrificed.

He must be returned to the spirit of the mountain."

It was not until they made to leave, that Bear became aware that the members of the hill tribe were now deliberately covering all the exit ways.

Small groups were on the entrance to the path, the beach and even up the mountain. Thorns and dense undergrowth barred the rest. And the tribespeople were armed with spears, axes and bows, not just the ceremonial kind.

Bear leaned forward to whisper a warning into James' ear. But as he moved, he suddenly gave a groan and clutching his stomach, fell forward into the dirt.

James suddenly realised that they were in trouble and just how much. He reached for Henry's shoulder, but then he too felt his vision blur. Soon, his lights dimmed as well and he slumped and slowly slid down his mage staff.

Only Henry remained on his feet.

Yet when he tried to move, the young man found that he couldn't. He was petrified, frozen to the spot. He could hear and he could see but could not act. It was like he was paralysed but conscious. Like a tarantula spider succumbing to the venom of the demon wasp.

Despite the fate of his father, what was unfolding around him and how he felt inside, he was able to see the winged visitor appear, land on a low branch and then "caw" excitedly.

"We have done your bidding," announced the treacherous shaman who had returned and was standing by Sunlance, the chief.

"Now we need you to speak with the mountain gods. We need you to request that they appease the angry ones and stem the fires, so we can return to living in peace."

Suddenly, without warning, the crow took off and flew at the Indian, raking at the eyes of the shaman, who only just managed to protect his face.

But the bird was powerful. While the shaman shrieked it was tearing at his hands with its iron beak.

"Please, please, forgive my rudeness, spare me," he screamed. Unanswered, he collapsed to his knees.

The cruel crow then flew back to the perch branch.

It stared with cold, dark, marbled eyes at the frozen but conscious Henry. Suddenly he feared what it could do to him, given he did not have the use of his limbs.

"Do not worry. We have used the lycanthra berry," said the shaman to the bird nervously as if reading their thoughts. "It is bad news for his changeling kind. The wolf in him will be paralysed for some time."

The bird started crowing what appeared to be a series of orders, and then it took to the air and soared to the top of the mountain.

The chief shouted and signalled to a couple of the men, who reluctantly wandered over and picked Henry up.

They carried him over to the totem pole then proceeded to tie him with his back to it. His eyes were nervously watching everything, terrified by an inability to do anything about their fate.

S till in brittle fae form, the captive sisters stared out through what looked like the iron bars of a filthy prison cell, into the interior of a room to which light was a ghostly stranger.

Thick layers of dust coated everything. It was of the type that has accumulated over decades of love lost, of neglect and inevitable decline.

Everything had happened so rapidly when they unceremoniously arrived, that it was all still a blur.

Their captive eagle had first circled what looked like a wooded and planted area with a few ramshackle buildings hidden in the shrubbery. Then it gave a low cry at receiving some sort of signal and swooped down at a chilling speed they could never hope to match. The great bird flew straight into this dismal place where they were blinded by a dark light then shoved unceremoniously into their cold prison by unseen digits or bony hands.

A strange, sort of red mist hung about the outside of the metal doors and grille, and the girls noticed that their precious magic items were somehow rendered dull and listless. The Rubyrobe was not emitting its usual warming, reassuring embrace. Helygenn would not appear and was shaking slightly in Alice's pocket where the Willowand sat like a cold bunch of brittle sticks gathered in the autumn and rattled by the wind.

In addition, the changeling sisters' magnificent, paper-thin wings were hanging limp and listless, and nothing crackled at the end of magical fingertips. Although what would happen if they suddenly morphed back into girls in such a confined space, probably didn't bear thinking about.

"This is bad," whispered Alice to her sister, her voice trembling a little and leaving a misty vapour trail.

Holly simply did her best to smile. She was wallowing in deep thought. Then she suddenly whipped off the cape and threw it at her sister.

Holly's actions were just in time as a spider, the size of a small dog, ran up Alice's back.

She then quickly bundled it into the Rubyrobe and sealed it off.

"Wha, wha, what was that?" Alice stuttered, looking visibly shocked and repulsed.

Holly held all the sealed ends and replied.

"Well, as we seem to still have our powers of animal language, this not-so minibeast may serve a useful purpose yet," she said, watching as the cloak bulged and rippled with the spider's struggles.

They waited until the palpitations became a little less frantic, then calmed to virtually still. Then Holly whispered, in her best, clicky arachnid tongue:

"That's better. Now, we mean you no harm. We are sorry we have invaded your home. But this was not of our making. I am going to let you free shortly. Still, you have to know that we are both powerful mages and you really don't want to mess with us again."

"Yeah. So, we need you to be nice," shouted Alice from behind her sister.

She paused for effect, then added, "Is that a deal?"

Holly waited some more, until gambling that she could take stillness as a sign of cooperation. Then, slowly, she unfolded the loops of her precious scarlet cloak until it revealed a dark shape. There, looking up as sheepish as it is possible for a bristly creature with several sets of eyes and long pointy fangs to look, was an unusually large, brown, female Canadian house spider. Despite her love of minibeasts, this beast was now maxi size. And it did creep her out a little. She couldn't help it.

Alice, on the other hand, the animal fanatic, was delighted to discover their housemate.

"Well, well, hello," she whispered, even extending her hand in a gesture of greeting which, reluctantly, the spider accepted, nervously pointing a couple of its long, hairy legs.

"You are not dinner size," she said, a note of sadness in her voice.

"Yet all the best bug-kind have scattered since SHE arrived," announced the spider, clearly annoyed.

"Now YOU squat in my house and this red barrier has been raised, frightening everything away. This whole house has started speaking in tongues that I have never heard. Gone is the peace we were born into. When will she leave? And when will you go and let the prey back in?"

Holly stroked her cheek, trying to think of the best way to win their companion over to their side. As ever, she chose kindness and reason.

"I am Holly, and this is Alice. We have been captured and brought here against our will. We too are unhappy, as we believe that the person you speak of means us all harm. Our family are nearby and will come to find us. But we're trapped in here and will need your help if any of us is to make it through this."

"I am named Hlilth," the pensive spider stated, in a voice that was like several people whispering at once and slurring their words with too many consonants.

"I am prepared to do what I can to return things to how they were. For I am hungry and am no friend of magicking. It offends against the natural order of things and always brings problems."

Holly and Alice swapped a knowing look at that wisdom, then Alice spoke up again.

"Are you still able to come and go as you please?"

"Of course. The red light is annoying, but it does not affect me. It just makes the other creatures afeared to enter this old oven, which makes them so much harder to catch."

"Oven?" repeated Alice.

"Yes, this is the oven, the cooking range. Although I think it has only been used to heat a pot or two since she invaded, which is annoying because when she lights it, I have to move and hide, again."

"So, she sometimes lights this oven up?" asked Alice again, her pupils widening.

"Well, only sometimes. Mostly she likes to use a big pot by the fireplace, which is always bubbling with something foul. Can't you smell that? That is a stew she made with some of my relatives, webs and all and other things she scavenged from the garden. I could hear her chopping up a poor bat the other night. And some frog spawn, boiled alive. Struggled terribly, they did."

She paused, waggling her dangling pedipalps between sentences.

"And they say spiders are cruel hunters. At least we inject our prey to send it to sleep. The things she has done are scandalous. Yes, yes, yes. We really want her gone. The things people say about spiders and wytches, they aren't true…."

Then she paused, recalling what the girls had said-"But hold on. You said earlier that you were…"

The girls looked at each other and shrugged.

"Well, we had to say something to get you to calm down. It was an exaggeration to call ourselves mages, to be fair."

Alice was amused to see her sister, usually so quick with the answers, struggling a little.

"But anyway," Holly added, dismissively, "back to the plan. If you can exit freely, could we perhaps trouble you to go and scout for us a bit? Let us know where she is, what she is doing and most importantly, what things she has with her?"

The spider was listening carefully, head tilting like an attentive

161

puppy.

"Of course. I can do that. May even happen upon a snack." At this her fangs twitched disturbingly and a little silver saliva venom appeared at the corners of her mouth.

"It is really important," repeated Holly. "We need to know all the details about anything she is making in the fire, items lying about that she has brought or harvested, markings she has made, especially candles, incense, crystals, things arranged into shapes. Can you do that for us?"

The spider appeared to nod and then, without further ado, she slunk through the rusty grille of what they now knew was the oven door and crawled down the length of the cast-iron leg.

Preparations for the fire dance ceremony were well underway by the time James and Bear recovered from the effects of the poison.

Neither could move, however. They had now been buried, up to their necks, side by side, in the soft sand. It was a simple, but classically effective form of confinement.

Fortunately for them, the sun had passed its highest point, its zenith and they were partially sheltered by a tree. But still, the golden orb's piercing rays were like sharp daggers in eyes that couldn't look away. Their skin was starting to colour and burn and both men were incredibly thirsty. The prospect of accepting another drink from the so-called medicine man, however, was not an appetising notion.

The trickster in the headdress was lurking conspiratorially with the tribal elders, clearly directing whatever he had planned for that evening.

The chief was nowhere to be seen, which didn't surprise him as he had a feeling that he was a good, if desperate man.

James could see his son strapped to the scorched totem pole in the middle of the ceremonial circle, piles of tinder carefully positioned around the circumference.

His heart sank when he realised that Henry wasn't moving. But when James made eye contact with him, he gave a surreptitious smile with his eyes to signal that he was still alive, at least. He was made of granite, that one.

James now turned to Bear, who was calmly trying to wriggle his shoulders free.

"Are you ok?" he whispered through gritted teeth.

He nodded, clearly embarrassed as well as frustrated.

"I cannot believe the extent of the treachery of these, an ancient tribe," he answered.

This was obviously both an insult and an embarrassment for the Indian. It was also incredibly uncomfortable for his sea-dwelling kind to be baked in the dry, abrasive sand so far removed from moisture.

"James, I must get out of this or…"

"I know. I know my friend," whispered James, conscious of his friend's merman needs yet calmly, aware that there were enemies everywhere.

"Things look bad. But once again, they underestimate us," James said, softly.

"We will get out of this. We simply have no other choice."

James may have been putting a brave face on matters, possibly fuelled by the hope that his wife and the rest of the family were making progress. Perhaps it was a blessing that he had no way of

164

knowing the truth about what was happening across the cold, dark sound.

Swift Hawk was now actually putting weight on his twice-damaged leg. He was walking in a circle, slightly uneasily and was amazed by the fact that the deep wound from the jaws of the trap appeared to be healing before their eyes.

"You are one powerful medicine lady," he said to Elouisa, as his confidence with the leg grew.

She simply smiled and teased in return, "It must have been that first aid kit from the boat. Those sprays work wonders."

Bill, whose cuts and bruises had also healed well, gave an ironic shrug. He had seen a lot in the last few days and had no doubt it wasn't over yet. But it was certainly a thrilling last chapter of an already fascinating story of a life on this frontier.

"If you think you can move again, we are certainly going to need you," Elouisa said.

Brinn noticed that she was now increasingly taking the lead. Her stature had changed. She held her head high. She was smiling more, despite their circumstances. And it warmed him to see the forces of light propping her up and holding back the terrible claim the darkness was trying to establish over her.

While they were resting, when not helping tend the stricken members of their party, Savannah had quietly taken a length of old-fashioned, thick-gauged rope from the boat and had left it soaking in the sea.

She had also commissioned a leaky old steel pail she had found by the ramshackle out house and had brought soothing salt water for her merman companion. To the amazement of the others, despite the bucket having large holes in it, it did not leak when she handled it.

Savannah had taken a timely soak in the shallows and now returned with the rope coiled about her waist.

While the others were preparing how best they could, Elouisa had walked slowly along the wisteria and creeper-covered archway they would need to navigate to reach the remains of the ramshackle dwelling they could see in the distance.

She had carved a range of runes on the bark of the thicker plants and placed crystals and bundles of twigs and feathers along the path.

Brinn too had joined with her in channelling some sort of force through the conducting items. The preparations had the feel of an ancient village preparing for some sort of military siege.

When the party finally finished their prep and gathered its resolve, setting off for the next stage in their quest, the warding spell kicked in. Collectively, they felt all their powers max out to full charge.

Savannah sighed beneath the glow of the Moonstone's gentle

force. Lucy stroked the Ravenring, which almost purred at her familiar touch and Brinn and Elouisa were visibly buoyed by the uplifting force of gentle light.

Interestingly, Hawk's beaded tribal necklace was now shining brighter than before. His magical spear tip glinted with a keen edge.

Bill, however, who was at the back of their small pack, watching for more unwanted guests, had to take assurance from the fact that he had his trusty rifle and a full magazine of shells. Perhaps he was standing a little taller? Perhaps the odd wrinkle had smoother itself or grey hair turned white. But he was characteristically nonplussed.

"Someone around here has to hold up the side of the normal folk," he muttered under his breath, while secretly relieved to be in such fine company.

"This dark magic was always here. Heaven knows how bad things would have gotten here had these special people not shown up when they did."

It was only a shortish walk of a few hundred metres down the covered walkway to the garden in front of the house. But it was dark, and dank and gloomy and creepy, and every step felt like a tramp through no-man's-land as if they were about to tread on a cursed land mine or another set of snapping metal jaws.

They were certainly right to be concerned.

Although the warding spell had held back the black magic that drained and suppressed their powers, the sea wytch held dominion over much of the Wiccan and Druidic worlds. She therefore commanded the obedience of those of nature's creatures she chose to enslave.

When they were about a third of the way down the tunnel of vegetation, Bill, bringing up the rear, the most vulnerable position, looked behind and a great eagle had landed on the stump Brinn had been sitting on earlier.

This was nothing too untoward until one by one, it was joined by others. Each was taking up vantage points on branches of the trees.

Now, it seemed, the very plants were coming to life. Creepers were slithering along ancient trellises and other supports like wire-bodied snakes, rippling sinuously in waves as they progressed. Meanwhile, all around them, they could hear growls, howls, cackles, spits and hisses, catching glimpses, between the vegetation and mist, of things, flying, running and jumping all around them as they pressed on.

"It sounds as I imagine hell does," said Bill, in his gently cracked voice, "but here on earth."

They were all being drawn variously into looking this way and then that, responding to unseen things that hit the bushes here or rattled the structure there, accompanied by what sounded like laughter. All felt the darkest and coldest of chills, except for Elouisa. The wytch remained resolutely focused on their destination and the inevitable encounter with destiny. She was mumbling some sort of incantation under her breath as she went and appeared to be surrounded by a cold, quiet fire.

A barbed paw flicked through the base of the walkway at one point, stabbing into Brinn's ankle. It wouldn't let go. Then something threatened to burst through behind it until Hawk stepped forward and discouraged it with his spear, sending it on its way with a howl of pain.

Brinn hobbled but continued, knowing how important it was for them to reach the end of this section of the journey through the dark garden.

Looking nervously over his shoulder, Bill could see that the eagles had gone from the end of the tunnel, clearly either unable to enter or considering it folly to do so. Given how cumbersome they are on land compared to the air, their dominion, they clearly had other plans.

Suddenly, a series of thuds on the foliage above them signalled the arrival of fresh terrors. Given there was not that much head clearance, claws started bursting through the gaps snatching at hair, hoods and aiming for faces while splinters and stones rained down.

They all crouched instinctively as they progressed, and Hawk and Bill lunged again and again, landing some lucky lustful blows.

The continuous screeching and screaming was deafening, as well as blood curdling.

Here and there, a feather fluttered through and Brinn snatched up a sample, placing them in the leather pouch about his waist.

The archway tunnel was only a flimsy vegetation barrier, but the plants held relatively firm. Whatever Wiccan enchantment Elouisa and Brinn had cast was largely holding fast, much to their relief.

As they reached the final stage of this journey within a journey, what waited for them at the end was something altogether more sinister.

As they drew closer, they could make out a shape that bore the size and markings of a slumbering grizzly. But it appeared listless, a bundle of former bear-life. It seemed to be half-seated, head tucked into its lap and chest.

Despite the cacophony of noise and the bedlam that had gone before, the inanimate shape remained impassive, not stirring. Yet ominously still it barred their exit and route to their final destination.

There, just behind the reeking hulk, with its door and two windows appearing like a tired and distorted face, waited the tired, bleached and ramshackle cottage. And as they all paused, struck dumb by how close they were, they caught their collective breath and contemplated what lay ahead. Few recognised that a deathly hush had now settled over the savage garden, a silence that was almost reverential.

Eventually, for several long moments, all they could hear was the rustling of the leaves on the feral trees. It was as if they were conspiring with the whispered sounds of the old house that creaked and groaned in the wind while it cooled in the late afternoon sun.

Holly squinted through the oven grille but still couldn't see very much.

Flickering light suggested candles. A powerful smell told her that incense was burning somewhere. She thought she could make out chalk markings on the floor but could not be sure.

However, a few minutes later their arachnid spy returned with a poor house cricket for dinner as well as a report.

"Well, she isn't actually in the house, not least so far as I can see. The wytch, that is. But there's sort of a crackling light around the door so I don't know if that's to keep things out or to keep things like you in."

"Did you see any large pointy drawings of symbols anywhere?" asked Alice, who had, after all, grown up in a wytch's lair and studied some lore.

"Well, there was a sort of web-shaped scratching on the floor but with sharp bits. It had pots all over it, some with powder, others salt, with lights in and one of them, a red one, was shining light up onto this oven."

"That's how she's created the remote magical field," said Alice. "If we can somehow snuff that candlelight, we'll at least be able to get out before…"

"Someone sparks up the fire?" asked Holly with a worried look.

"Exactly. Hlilth, can you think of any way to turn over that red candle jar?"

"Hm!" The spider was thinking, stroking its face with two spidery legs.

"There is a family of rats living in here, in the wall cavities. They have a habit of eating we minibeasts. But I'm faster than most."

Holly was grinning.

"Well, if you could potentially get it to chase you and then sort of run…"

The spider went quiet.

"You're asking me for a lot. Your plan is filled with danger. What's in it for me?"

Alice chipped right back with, "Not being boiled alive by the sea wytch and getting your house back maybe?"

But Holly wanted a more measured response.

"We are a magical family with all sorts of gifts and abilities. So why don't you let us know how we can help?"

"Yes, name your price," her sister added, gruffly.

The spider thought again.

"I want my own place. A really messy, dusty, bug infested place that no two-legged barbarians will ever visit, (no offence) and where our babies can grow! Deal?"

"Is that all?" spluttered Alice, until Holly nudged her.

"Deal!" said Holly, giving her sister a dirty look.

"Babies?" she added.

"Yes. But just a hundred dozen hatchlings, up there in the back corner," the spider pointed.

When the girls looked closely, they could see hundreds of sets of eyes, like their own star cluster or constellation.

"Right," said the spider, "I better get on with it," and with that she skuttled off and abseiled out again, better than any SAS soldier.

The sisters waited anxiously.

But eventually they could make out an excited squeak, scuffling and the noise of small feet pattering fast. The plan was clearly working out.

Suddenly, they heard a sort of crunch but then the distinctive sound of glass on wood. And then the red light suddenly dropped.

"She's done it. Really looks like she's done it."

Alice was most excited and rushed to the grille. Now she could push her arm through, then squeeze her head.

She felt a nudge and heard a yawn, and Helygenn popped his head out of her breast pocket, stars puffing from his nose.

He then casually popped between the grille sections, and without being asked somehow got the latch of the oven to lift. The whole heavy door then swung open with a terrible creak.

Holly cringed at the sound, worried they may be heard and ushered Alice out quickly. They both then tried their wings which had regained some of their vigour. Despite feeling like pins and

175

needles they were delighted to see that they worked well.

As they flew down to the overturned jar, they were startled to see a pair of red eyes staring at them from a hole by the wall.

Alice whispered to Helygenn to stand watch as they searched the floor. He smiled a tiny dragonny smile, clearly happy to be busy and flew into the hole at speed, breathing a small stream of steam to a chorus of squeaking, and scrabbling for safety all about them.

The girls searched frantically for their brave arachnid friend. But it wasn't until they looked inside the jar that they learned her fate.

To their horror, trapped beneath the glass, they could see a long leg, twitching weakly.

It seemed that when the rat had pounced, the glass had rolled onto the spider in a freakish accident.

They rolled the glass back off the missing legs. But the damage had seemingly already been done.

She was now dragging herself pitifully into the corner. Sadly, her delicate abdomen was damaged beyond the help of any magic. Even the soothing touch of the Rubyrobe was not enough, despite Holly laying a corner of it upon her tenderly in an effort to bring some comfort.

Tears welled up in the girls' eyes. These turned into sobs when they heard her attempts to muster a few final words.

As they both kneeled, all they could make out were a few words in a muffled whisper, "Babies. You faeries make sure you remember your promise to my children."

Brinn held his arm out, a gesture suggesting the small group pause with caution.

He then drew his golden sickle from his cloak and approached the raggedy bear very slowly.

Elouisa made as if to accompany him, but with a gesture he ushered her back.

He got to within a couple of feet of the danger before he detected any signs of life.

At first, he thought it was the noise of snoring, a sort of low, rhythmic hum. But then he realised that it wasn't snoring. It was some sort of repetitive word pattern, a type of chant.

"But there is something wrong here," he thought.

Before his brain could process the fact that it wasn't chanting in the Brunish, the language of the bears, the situation deteriorated rapidly.

Rising to its full height, the grizzly bear came to life. Well, it sort of came to life, as one look at its dusty, raggedy, moth eaten pelt gave an important clue to its true nature. For this bear was no living animate object, it was some sort of undead beast, a mummified pelt brought to zombie life by dark forces.

The dark magick monster stumbled toward the elderly Druid with a sort of crippled shambling gait. It didn't growl or snarl.

All that could be heard was the voice of the necromancer's chant, rising and falling in volume as it gave its evil commands from somewhere, a tone rising above the over-powering stench of aged carrion.

Brinn stepped back a couple of paces to create thinking space. Then, with a sweeping wave of his free hand over the curved blade, he lit the small scythe with blue, magical flame.

Were this any normal opponent, especially an animal, that action would be enough to terrify it. But this was no ordinary beast. It simply pressed further forward, arms flailing and jaws snapping.

Brinn continued to lure the abomination away from the others, walking swiftly backward, his intention to trick it into following him down to the sea where they had the advantage. But just as his plan was working, his naked sandalled foot felt the soft touch of a pile of leaves. Before thought met action, something hard and cold was fast followed by another searing strike of angry steel jaws.

"Aaaaggghh!" he screamed, as the wretched rusty man-trap bit into his delicate, aged calf, skin and bone.

When he inevitably fell over backward, the ghoulish grizzly marched forward relentlessly. Brinn could smell its rotting pelt as it was virtually upon him, yet he had the presence of mind to have held onto his sickle. With a backward, slicing swing the Druid cut into its exposed belly, and as he did, the flames caught quickly on the aged fur.

But despite being alight and cut from west to east, the grizzly zombie was seemingly undeterred. It loomed down at the old man, stinking.

Then the cavalry arrived.

Feeling their powers return, Lucy was the first to react. Pressing the ring, she sent a flock of bats at the rotting head of the beast.

This confused and stalled it enough for Savannah to reveal the weapon she had furnished for this very purpose.

The water in the soaked rope enabled her to control it, like a pet python. Like a coiled cable, she sent the thick rope hissing across the lawn. Soon it was whipping around the standing limbs of the shambling abomination.

This eventually caused it to stumble and then fall face down onto the lawn. The flames were now licking about its rotten body. But not before Bill had got a couple of shots off into its body, tearing away large chunks of fetid flesh.

This then left Hawk to administer the coup de grâce, or killing blow with his deadly, shining spear. He charged, lunged, struck and then tore a huge gaping wound as deep as it was wide, snapping fossilised bones.

Elouisa could see that they had matters in full control. So she was now attending to her father who was in considerable pain, even when she removed the biting jaws of the trap, once again using the Athame dagger.

She had retained much of the poultice they had used earlier and while the others cleared up the remnants of the zombie, she soothed and bound the wound. But looking at the jaws of the trap, she detected some sort of foreign agent and her heart dropped.

"Foxglove?" asked her father, knowing the answer.

"It looks that way. But I'm sure…" her voice trailed off.

"You are many amazing things, my daughter. But sadly, you are no match for your mother's dark alchemy. It comes with the curse of spite and a hatred you can't overcome or hope to match."

As he spoke, she could see that he was already looking very pale and tinged with green around the side of his face.

He was clutching his heart now and croaked, weakly, "Feels like mambaweed to me."

"No," said Elouisa, far too swiftly.

"There is no known antidote. We both know that."

"I will find a way, Father," she said, as the others gathered round.

Hawk could see, straight away, that this was a very different situation to the one he had just recovered from.

"We need the Rubyrobe. We need Holly," said Lucy, holding her grandfather's hand, trying to comfort him.

Elouisa was attempting to call James but his mobile phone went straight to voicemail.

"They're too far away, no signal, I can't get through…"

Brinn was now coughing, badly, a rasping, rattling noise. Blood splatters appeared on the front of his light, now grey robe, and Elouisa could see that his breathing was becoming increasingly laboured.

"Holly, we need Holly," repeated Lucy, giving voice to their combined feelings, increasingly frantic as the dark snake's poison tightened its grip.

Savannah took hold of her sister's hand; she then took hold of Elouisa's and completed the chain.

As they did so, all their magical artefacts started to glow. The light green flowed from them and along the arms of the party, an emerald pentagram of love.

Lucy held one of her grandfather's hands and Savannah the other, until the glow flowed into the old man. Slowly, much like a pan on a fire bubbles, his breathing became stronger and eventually, he opened his tired eyes, the pain still very much in evidence.

"No children please," he whispered in a weak voice. "Listen to me. It is my time now. You must let me go. Focus on safety. Look to the rest of the family. This venom can't be contested, not even by its maker."

The sun was on top of the fiery mountain now, signalling a quarter of an hour until dusk. It glowed burnished orange against the iron-ore coloured cloud of effluent it was belching out, an ominous signal that the end of days was nigh.

From the preparations they had witnessed, whatever the mountain tribe had been planning would be happening shortly.

Bear was still conscious but was clearly suffering a great deal, his every pore bleeding life force into the thirsty sand.

Henry, however, for anyone who could read his body language, seemed to be growing in strength. He had the look of a patient predator, scanning for weaknesses, biding his time.

Gradually, the tribal members, braves, women and children took up bespoke places between the now lit fires around the circle.

The tribal medicine man joined the visiting shaman and together they performed a dancing incantation, an orchestration of spirits. They were singing and wielding war hammers and staffs, intermittently spitting coloured fluid from a buckskin gourd on the ground around the circle, an action that lit up the whites of their wide eyes.

In the gloom, somewhere, a group of drummers maintained a steady rhythm like a heartbeat. Then gradually the assembled crowd began a low, slow, hypnotic chant.

"What are they singing?" James asked his now groaning partner, trying to distract him from the torment he was clearly in as his sensitive skin roasted.

"This is not good," he croaked a cracked reply.

"They are calling for the spirit god, Amotken. They are talking of sacrifice, blood-letting to liberate the land."

James could now make out the words,

"Amotken, Amotken, Amotken," then, "rise again, rise again."

This rhythmic chanting was building and climbing to a promised crescendo as more of the tribe joined in and the antics of the medicine men became increasingly animated in reply.

The tribal shaman was now spitting fire, igniting a fluid he was drinking from a decorated flask.

A group of warriors stepped forward and placed a larger gourd of presumably the same liquid in front of the totem and Henry.

The sun had now set completely, but it was still surprisingly light. The place of the orange ball in the sky had been taken by a portentous full moon, glowing an incredible luminous blue as it appeared over the line of the trees. This light gave the whole scene an otherworldly feel as if the distance between the veils between magic and human kingdoms had become paper thin.

The two medicine men were now dancing just a couple of feet away from Henry, the length of the totem pole lit up by the firebrands they both carried. The snarling and threatening faces of the creatures carved into the ancient tribal totem artefact leered aggressively, even protectively. But nothing, it seemed, had power enough to prevent the dark events that were threatened next.

Two of the warriors raised the decorated gourd above the head of the restrained boy. They then slowly emptied its contents, pouring the liquid all over him, soaking him from head to toe.

James could see that he was clearly blinking and gasping for air as the thick, stinging fluid invaded his eyes, nose and mouth. But still, there was no panic from their son.

"Be strong my son," he called, but was silenced by a hard blow to the head.

The chanting of the tribal members now rose to an almost frenzied climax, the drumming increasing in volume, driving it on.

"Amotken, Amotken, Amotken, rise again, RISE AGAIN!"

Then the tribal witch doctor and his visiting accomplice looked to the tribal chief as they danced before Henry, torches raised.

At this point, unexpectedly, Henry lifted his head, looked to his father, then followed the eyes of the shaman.

The chief raised his war lance, eagle feathers catching the moonlight. He then brought it sharply down.

It was the signal.

The shamans turned to each other, then walked forward ominously to set fire to the flammable liquid covering Henry. But as their torch light lit up his face, maniacal grins morphed to fear and they shrieked an alarm. Henry, the boy, had now gone.   It was Henry the wolf now strapped to the pole. His fur resisted the attention of the flames and he clearly had no intention of being confined for much longer.

With a roar, he first snapped the bonds as if they were soft twine.

Then with two sharp and mighty blows, with paws ablaze, he floored the medicine men, frozen with abject fear.

At this point, all hell broke loose around the circle as emboldened by his arrival, first the wolves came snarling to his aid. They were followed closely by Bear's tribe, their coastal Salish companions.

Throughout the circle, hand to hand battles were being fought in the dark and half shade. A cacophony of growls, snarls, screams of fear and agony and furious battle cries filled the night air.

Some of the mountain tribe fled to the centre, trying to escape the dark terrors in the shadows on the fringes. But they too were fast overcome.

A terrifying sight, fur ablaze in parts, Henry sought out the treacherous medicine man and pinned him to the ground. Surprisingly, he was able to vocalise in a manner this pitiful man monster could understand:

"You, you are the trickster, the double-dealer, the sycophant most hated of all legends. Now it is time for you and your kind to pay for your crimes."

But as Henry brought his terrifying face within millimetres of their enemy, he saw a sudden flash light up the man's pupils. Simultaneously, most of the fighting Indians were floored by a thundercrack, like the mighty whip of a god.

When he turned and looked up, lightning was still striking the totem pole, streaking through torrential rain and hail.

But what every onlooker was in awe of wasn't the destructive power of this lance of the spirit gods that ripped down from the mountain. What they were stunned by was the fact that, when the smoke cleared, far from being destroyed, the totem pole appeared refreshed, renewed.

The colours and expressions of the mythological beings had come to life, as if carved and painted yesterday. But terrifyingly, they were moving, eyes staring, mouths gaping, and teeth bared.

Yet all eyes were now drawn to the top of the totem. As Henry stood up, in lycanth form, lifting the shaman up by his lying mouth, he was silhouetted against the blue moon over the mountain, the rain and the smoke adding depth and drama.

Several feet above his seven-foot height, however, was a fresh carving.

This had not been made by any master carver of the clans.

This had been created by the very gods themselves.

And what it showed was a ferocious beast, half man and half wolf.

It was a very special type of changeling.

But much more than that, it was quite clearly a carving of Henry.

Atop this important totem pole, in the priority position, was a depiction of what was now the most intimidating changeling, the alpha, the walking god.

As James and Bear stared on, still trapped in the ground, the scene enacted on central stage stunned them.

Every member of the two tribes fighting here had now dropped silently to their knees.

They were now prostrating themselves. Not before the totem or some mountain god, but before his son. Before Henry.

A deathly hush had settled over the clearing, as the werebeast held the arched body of the medicine man aloft in a single hand.

Then Henry threw back his own head and howled a primal scream. He was soon joined by the entire wolf pack, a collective cacophony until, in reply, the thunder clapped, echoing accord around the mountain.

Henry and the wolves serenaded the moon like no one had ever done before. And his father and everyone within the valley felt the force. It was like the primal side of the changeling was rebelling against what man had done here, as if the boy had joined the animal kingdom to protest, from his very soul.

C onfident that they had broken the dark wytch's barrier spell of control but concerned at what else she may have planned to take advantage of their unique powers, the girls resumed their human form. Somehow, they felt they could handle her more easily as grandchildren rather than competitors and threats.

"Not so easy to get us into the oven now, anyway," said Holly, as Alice carefully placed the body of the spider in her pocket.

Helygenn had returned from the hole in the wall, looking rather smug at having banished the rats for good. He was soon back in Willowand form and snug in Alice's pocket like a magical marsupial.

The girls stepped gingerly around the pentangle on the floor, scattering the crystals and runes as they trod on the floorboards. All the candles had been extinguished when the power chain had been broken, setting them free.

Crossing to the door, every creaking plank set off alarm bells in their heads, made worse by over-active imaginations that turned shadows into demons.

So, they were surprised when Holly turned the handle and the door creaked open without anything more abusive or malevolent than the last of the daylight stinging causing them to blink and shield their eyes.

As they were adjusting to the open air after a lengthy confinement in the dirt and the dust, a call from the corner of the garden caught their attention.

"Lucy!" Alice shrieked and then ran over to her sister, seeing the rest of the family group who had left with her gathered in a semi-circle.

"What's wrong?" she asked, seeing her face.

Holly arrived as she spoke and whisked her sister up into her arms. But she too became quickly aware that there was a problem.

Then they saw him, the old man, prostrate on the grass, face as grey as his clothing, his beard spattered with blood.

Lucy was crying. "He has been poisoned, Holly," she sobbed. We've tried but he's slipping away."

Holly crouched down and tenderly interrogated their grandfather's face.

He couldn't speak anymore, but he did manage the makings of a kindly but weak smile.

Without thinking, Holly scrunched up alongside the ancient Druid and draped him in her Rubyrobe. She then reached for Alice's hand, who sat down with her, the rest of the group creating a full circle around him.

The sun had now set, yet the magical glow from and within the circle could be clearly seen.

"We will remain like this for as long as it takes to chase that foulness from your blood and system, Grandad," said Holly.

"If we can retain this contact and focus, I know I can track and trace it through his system." As she said this, Alice felt a nudge in her chest and, sure enough, Helygenn wriggled free. This time, he was a stunning jade-coloured snake and slithered swiftly down her arm and onto the old man's chest.

Helygenn always had a mind of his own, but they were not expecting his next move. For the snake reared up, exposed his fangs and sank them deep into the main artery in the old man's neck.

Lucy was shocked and made as if to try to remove the serpent, but was stopped by their Indian companion.

"No. Wait. You must not break the circle. All that slithers is not evil-kind. Look," he implored.

The tip of Helygenn's tail was gradually darkening. This was no attack. It was a sign that he was sucking out that which was attempting to claim her grandfather's soul.

The longer he worked, the more the colour changed.

Very slowly, the opposite was happening with the Druid. Ever so gradually, signs of the bloom of life showed in his cheeks.

"We must hold this connection," shouted Holly. "It's working, but we mustn't break the current."

"NO, YOU MUST NOT!" cackled a rasping voice, emerging from the darkness behind the tree against which Brinn rested and around which the group were gathered. The unexpected softness of that voice was more terrifying than if it had come in a thunderclap.

"Hello, daughter!" the sea wytch called, mockingly. "Thought you could abandon me? Leave me alone? Thought I would simply shrivel up and die?"

Elouisa could feel her heart racing. But she knew that she had to remain calm for the sake of the children, remain calm and "THINK".

"His weakness was always his love. His demise would always be his empathy. He dared to come hunting. WELL, look who is shrivelling and dying now."

And with that she broke into a high-pitched cackling laugh-scream that echoed around the garden then fled down to the sea.

Clad completely in jet-black robes, she shuffled slowly around the back of the circle. She paused behind each of them, so close to flesh that they could feel her fetid breath touch the hairs on their neck or the prickle of the long wires on her nose and chin.

To make matters worse, they soon realised that she was not unaccompanied. They heard and smelled it long before they saw it. For sitting upon her shoulder, snuffling like the pig demon it is, was her new familiar, her wytch's pet.

Yes, the nemesis of the family was now accompanied by the African imp, the maggot with sharp teeth, the odious Tokoloshe.

And judging by the way it was dribbling and snuffling and gnashing its jagged teeth, it had not been properly fed since they left the Namibian desert.

The wolf pack were quick to cluster around Henry, forming a protective cordon that he probably didn't need. For it was clear to everyone gathered about that totem pole that the changeling was related to the spirits, to the powerful deities that they believed shaped their earth.

All that moved on two feet or four was now deeply in awe of the wereboy.

The only members of the tribe moving were those desperately and meekly digging James and Bear from their sand cages upon the command of the Salish chief.

Bear was in a terrible state when they finally got him out and had to be carried to the river to totally immerse and recover.

James took a drink and poured half over his head. But he was more concerned about approaching his son.

The wolves, however, barred his way threateningly when he entered the circle and although he could call upon his magic and force a path, he was very reluctant to ignite the charged atmosphere, especially as weak as he felt.

Then Henry growled a command.

James' eyes never left those of his son as he walked forward. But he could feel from his very aura that something fundamental had shifted, their relationship had changed.

Before James could speak, it was apparent that the usually introverted and softly spoken boy had clearly undergone some sort of transformation. It just felt right that James waited for Henry to take the initiative, this time.

"Father, for you will always be known as my father, we have very little time. The others are in grave danger and we have much work yet to do."

The sentence asked more questions than it answered for James, but he consoled himself with the fact that Henry still identified as his son.

There was a very different look in his eye now and a certainty in his manner.

"I can feel that our mother is in trouble, terrible trouble. That can only mean that the dark one has been found and she is continuing her quest for dominion over this family and now this land. If we do not get to them soon, land, people, sea and sky, all will be lost."

With this, Henry signalled to the pack. In a matter of minutes, they had assembled and set off down the forest path at a fast run. Without further questioning, James reached for his snake staff and with some trouble and a lot of concentration, settled in behind the pack. Henry was easily outpacing the fastest of the wolves and was soon leading from the front.

Despite the dark of the night, James noticed, up above, shadowing their progress, a large-winged corvid soaring just above the trees. The full moon glinted off its lustrous feathers, implying silver and blue mercury and James toyed with the notion of bringing it down. Then he realised that this time, the double-tongued one's treachery might just work in their favour.

When they entered the deep part of the rainforest, the crow could no longer keep up, so it peeled off and headed across the sound.

James knew he would fly straight to the sea wytch, which would forewarn her. But it may also just distract her and buy them some time.

Blessed with night vision, the wolves deftly leaped over moss-laded logs, clumps of rocks, pools and streams. Henry led, as if he had always lived here and knew every leaf of fern or blade of grass. He maintained a punishing pace, but the pack were built for it and all around him, James could hear rhythmic pants and the pounding of paws. So he focused on remaining in the middle, letting dozens of eyes see for him.

In what seemed like no time, they arrived at the altar rock and waiting for them was a sight that took James' breath away. Dark shapes in the water revealed a virtual flotilla of orcas, several pods of killer whales packed into the bay. They also responded to Henry's primal call as if it were part of a greater plan unfolding.

More than that, waiting just beyond the break water was nothing other than Captain Bill's beautiful blue boat, the Okwaho.

The wolves didn't stop at the beach. What followed was the bizarre sight of wolves leaping over the waiting whales and swimming strongly for the boat. The whales moved in behind as many of them as they could and gently steered them through currents on their way.

James, of course, was able to ride his staff across the short stretch of water and had the presence of mind to unlock the landing deck at the rear, in readiness for the influx to come.

Henry was first, not swimming but riding on the back of the dominant bull whale, and he leaped onto the deck as deftly as a marine mammal.

James was now trying to put his mind to how to operate the boat, when it struck him that, by rights, Okwaho should still be the other side of the sound.

All the wolves now appeared to be aboard, and the air was thick with spray as they shook themselves dry, sending a cloud of wet dog up to the bridge where James was preparing to start the engine.

But before he could, he noticed that they were on the move. Yet he could hear no propeller.

Moving tentatively to the side, the water was virtually black all the way round the boat. The orcas were now powering the craft and were making short work of the crossing, achieving a rate of knots that was alien to the veteran ship.

James couldn't suppress a bit of a grin at this whale equivalent of horsepower for cars, but then the opposite shore came into view and his mind returned to the earnest matters at hand.

He could see that smoke was rising from what appeared to be a factory chimney, but oddly it was a strange shade of ochre.

"That can only mean one thing", James thought. "Mohbreen must already be there".

"She is father, I feel her," said Henry, as if reading his very thoughts now.

"But what is about to come will settle things one way or another, for good."

James noted that he had not resumed his human form and seemed completely steady and comfortable in his alternative skin, something that had not always been the case in the past. He was also speaking in lycanth. This night was a night of firsts, and it wasn't over yet.

Without thinking, he reached out his hand and tenderly caressed his son's strong, lupine jaw.

Their eyes met in a prolonged moment of intimate affection, in which James could see himself reflected in his son's deep, dark eyes.

But then the boat came to a halt, as they had clearly reached the beaching area and the moment passed.

James had to avert his face for a few seconds and run the back of his hand across his eyes.

Instinctively, he somehow knew that that was their final moment as father and child. And although he looked on with pride as Henry commanded his pack, the former male and female alphas hanging on his every word, part of him wilted at the moment's passing, part of his heart chilled, never again to be revived.

The sea wytch was fuelled by the tension she caused with every word, every move, every gesture. She had lived for so long, for the great pleasure of feeding off this control. And with every new addition to the mongrel Trelgathwin line, those Savages, the sweeter was the scale of her inevitable revenge.

"I have awaited this moment with growing appetite," she hissed, like a boiling pot.

"You knew there would be a price to pay for diluting our Celtic blood, rebel daughter. Had I not myself torn you from my own womb, I would have doubted our very kinship. For you were, are and remain so, so pitifully feeling, so very weak."

She noticed that the children tried to conceal their interest, but still hung on her every word.

As dark had fallen like a great theatre curtain, the glow that spilled from the family circle started to pick out dozens of marble onlooking eyes glinting in the darkness. Here, in the shade, untold terrors were awaiting their mistress' command.

Then, with a theatrical flourish, something blocked out the blue moon for a second. It was the treacherous crow flying in from the west.

"So," said the crone, "what message do you have for me, fork-tongued spy? When will I get my hands upon the neck of the wretched Cornishman?"

"Eminence," cawed the crow. "He does not journey alone. He is now at the head of a lupine army."

But she didn't stop to listen, cackling out her disdain with a chilling cry, "Wolves?" she mocked. "Mere wolves? What? Will they sprout wings and fly here like you? Or perhaps they will grow flat tails like beavers instead and swim across between the teeth of the killer whales, sent mad by the fumes from my majestic mountain?"

The crow paused, tilting its head as if weighing each sentence with great care:

"Nevertheless, your dark majesty, they are on their way. You don't und…"

But she cut the crow off in mid-sentence.

"Well, let them, let them come." She cackled again, waiving her arms in a bony display of white, sagging skin. "Those who do not become food for the crazed blackfish will be fed to my ever-hungry wild cats or enraged bears. They are waiting here so patiently, terrible beauties all." At this, she gestured towards the spotlights in the darkness, glowing everywhere.

"YOU would like to play with the pussies, wouldn't you little one," she teased, inserting a long talon into Alice's neck until it leaked. "Aw, she so loves the bubba animals, doesn't she?"

She let out a dry, raucous laugh like expelling gas.

"You may want to attack me, little tiger-cat, but you should know that none of my progeny can really do me harm. None of the descendants of my bloodline can end my reign of pain. Yes, I have bred iron armour into your very genes."

This had the desired effect. Alice's famous temper was fraying, and she could feel the heat of her anger rash rising up her neck.

"I HATE you!" she spat.

"Don't let her provoke you, Alice," Elouisa countered in a whisper. "The cruelty feeds her."

"Whatever we do, we must hold the circle until your father returns, he will pass and she will pick us off, one by one."

The wytch was circling the vulnerable group now. The crow watched as if fascinated, its head tilted this way, then that, conscious that it had been cut short and not finished the full report.

The crone almost wandered past Lucy. But then she noticed something move at the base of her neck. Lucy's little skeleton familiar had made a mistake that would prove terminal. It had tried to look into the eyes of one similar to its creator.

With a surprisingly deft move, the sea wytch snatched up the tiny creature. It wriggled for a second. Then she grinned and threw it to the hungry Tokoloshe.

Before horrified eyes, the beast polished it off with a couple of crunches, like so much stale beef jerky.

"Noooooooo!" screamed Lucy and Alice simultaneously. They

were both sobbing. But to their great credit, they did not let go, the circle remained intact.

The odious hag smiled, showing black teeth. She then moved slowly on and stopped by Holly this time.

"Ah, the diddums didn't let go. And what about you? Always the teacher's pet. Forever Little Miss Right. So like your father. But I broke him. It was simple. I just used you as a torture tool," she snarled.

"But no matter how hard you kick that Cornish vermin, like the undead, he just rots and refuses to give up."

"Have you not considered the things old Granny can teach you? I know you believe you are better than them. Well, I can show you how to control weaklings rather than suffer them. You don't have to beat them all. Just use them. The darker tricks of magick could be yours and will mean you will always win, no matter what." She spoke as if in an intimate whisper, yet for all to hear.

"I would rather lose than follow you!" Holly shouted in a louder voice than expected. But she almost let her grip go as she did and reined herself back in again when she realised that she was being played for a fool.

The wytch cackled. Then tutted loudly.

"Shame. Such passion could be used for much more productive things," the wretched woman whispered, the wart on her chin touching the side of Holly's face, which recoiled involuntarily.

"Join me. All you have to do is let go. So simple. Relax into it and be done with that burden of goodness forever, child. There is a force in you much stronger than your mother."

This time the sea wytch stuck out her snake-like tongue, and Hawk, who was opposite. recoiled as he could see that it was cleft in two like a reptile's.

"Axwadus the child eater. Foul-faced Basket Ogress," he spat under his breath.

She noticed his reaction.

"Ah, the cripple Indian brave. Have you tried getting back into the water, fish boy? Who knows what that muck was she splattered on you? The apple does not fall far from the tree, you know. There is way too much more of me in this one than him."

She now sniffed Hawk's hair, making a loud exhaling noise and then, much to his disgust, ran her forked tongue up the side of his face, tasting his sweat.

"Mmmmmm! The undeniable tang of fear and hate." She then cackled again, deep into his ear, making his very soul shiver.

He was forced to kick out with a lightly sandalled foot as the foul creature accompanying her was snuffling about his toes. It gave a sort of whimpering growl but tried to come back for more, and he felt the prickle of one of its tusks before he landed a better blow. This sent it scurrying back up the body of its adopted mistress crying like a pup.

Meanwhile the wytch's left hand started to stroke the hair of her daughter. It was a mocking motion, as if tenderly brushing her mid-length, mousy locks.

"So unspectacular a girl. So plain a beta woman. So mediocre as a witch. Such a disappointment." She cackled cruelly, like the bully she was.

"It is as if someone set out to assemble the very runty middle part of a middle pack and made the recipe from you. Racked by self-doubt. Paralysed by fear. Destined to be nothing without stealing from others."

She now had one of her talons trained on her daughter's head, the other was clutching at her heart. It was as if she was pulling strings of doubts and fears, reading them and returning them with interest.

But when she tried to thrust home her final point, she hit something hard in her daughter's chest and withdrew her claw with a curse.

"Aaaagh," she swore, having snapped a long, sharp talon-like nail.

"How can you end up being not quite anything? Was it HIS dusty seed? Why, even your blind sister is…"

But she got no further, as suddenly the tree around which they were gathered lit up with a blue roaring light.

The sea wytch made no sound but recoiled several feet, thrown backward to the ground by a tremendous force.

A deafening noise, like a clap of thunder left all their ears ringing.

But when they looked up expectantly, this was no act of any god. For none other than Old Bill looked back down at them. He was wearing a frightened but determined look on his face. And both barrels of his shotgun were now smoking.

Wild cats of all varieties normally recoil and run from the sound of a human's fire stick. But these creatures were so bewitched by the summoning charm the wicked crone had brewed up in the cottage and scattered around the garden, that they would have run through flames just to be at her side.

So rather than retreat, the blast had the opposite effect and from every part of the garden, mountain lions or cougars were joined by errant, snarling black bears, all now converging on the circle of humans.

Like Cougar-Annie had once done at this very spot, Bill was firing indiscriminately between any spot where he saw two orange lights, or sets of eyes. But he was one, and they were many.

Without breaking the circle, Savannah, Moonstone glowing like the falling star it was, muttered an enchantment of her own. Beautiful head tossed back, she commanded the rope, still coiled about the feet of the body of the zombie, to rise up and spin like a propeller blade. It had less water in it now, but still responded. This did the job of protecting their open flank, as no beast would now approach for fear of losing life or limb.

It also bought them just enough time for the grey wolf pack to disembark as one and sprint up from the beach.

Suddenly Cougar-Annie's garden became a battle ground of native beasts. Ancient ancestors of cat and dog-kind were fighting one-on-one contests everywhere, their snarls and screams filling the night.

The family circle held fast throughout the melee. Brinn was finally starting to show some signs that he may be winning his personal battle and looking down, Elouisa noticed that the wand-serpent had almost turned colour completely, the still-spreading darkness a mark that most of the poison had been drained.

As she looked up again, none other than her beloved James was flying towards her. He dismounted and spinning his staff deftly on his hands, dispatched an enchanted black bear, which had made the mistake of rearing up in his path.

Felling it with two blows, he slipped straight into his stride, firing a stream of fire from the tip of his staff to create a path through to his family. Upon his arrival he dipped into a crouch and sent a stream of stars into the undergrowth, teasing a crowd of creepers into life to form a barrier around much of the tree. A couple of cougars were swept up into the bullying branches, tendrils muzzling the beasts while holding them fast.

Eyes blazing, enraged by what he saw, James responded to his wife's imploring, urgent gaze and crossed to their fallen foe. In a double-handed blow, he brought his staff down on the body of the prostrate sea wytch, hidden somewhere in that black bundle of rags that had borne the brunt of the shotgun blast.

But he was shocked when his raging violence did not meet the flesh-like resistance he anticipated.

When he turned to his wife holding up the empty clothing, the desperate look on her face said everything. The despair was too much for her to bear and she let her arms drop.

"No, no, no! I should have known," she cried. "I would have known, have felt it had the shot truly taken her.

"She has gone. She's escaped justice once again."

James searched the area frantically then noticed a familiar body shape. There, thrown to one side and onto its back, on the floor, a look of stunned shock still frozen on its face, was the odious Tokoloshe. Her familiar had taken the fatal blast for the crone. The demon's destiny had finally been fulfilled a long way from its African roots. And its final act was to spell more disaster.

Brinn, at this point began to cough and splutter like a drowning man plucked from the water and thrown onto the beach.

Helygenn, in reptile form, had detached and now slithered off into the darkness to be violently ill. The poison was deeply unpleasant, and it needed to be purged from the system.

The children were frozen, horrified. Their hands were still together. But their mother's hands lay limply by her sides.

As had been predicted by the were wytch, her daughter had fulfilled her fate. She had broken the circle. And despite the efforts of their father to comfort her, there was nothing more they could do. In stunned silence, they could but look on as the last of the colour faded from Brinn's cheeks. Then, with a light groan, a weak smile and a long last breath, there, at the centre of his family, the ancient druid finally crossed over.

Whatever happens," James whispered, calmly, "we will find her. And justice will follow close behind."

There was considerably less noise from around the garden now, which accentuated the children's desperate sobbing.

The undead army had withdrawn, thankfully, or in this moment of weakness they could well have succumbed.

The wolves were grouping back together and re-bonding after the battle, as only those animals do, licking wounds, congratulating and grooming each other while sharing stories of their individual contests. There seemed to be plenty of injuries, some more serious than the battle scars others would brag about. But in the main they were back in one piece and it seemed, by their behaviour, their losses were thankfully few.

The loss of Brinn would echo through the generations but as his wife lapsed into inconsolability, what now troubled James most, was that there was no sign of Henry.

Holding Lucy's hand which was wet with her tears, he gently escorted his daughter for a quiet word with Ice Eye, the alpha female. She was nursing a bear-bite on her partner's shoulder.

"The pack were excellent," said James, in his best lupine language, "truly a force to be reckoned with. Thank you."

"Given your great loss, your words carry even more weight," she said, with sympathy. "But do you know what became of the spirit god?"

James was disappointed, as he had clearly hoped for an answer to the same question.

Then, from above them, a voice like a strangled bullfrog pierced the trepidation.

"Look to the boat. The changeling has returned to the mountain but is not travelling alone."

Then with a raucous "caw, caw", Nubia took off again, clearly jeering, laughing, mocking.

"He is not alone…never alone. Destiny awaits. Never alone."

The collective mood had no triumphalism about it and was made worse by the crow's announcement.

Looking round his shattered friends and family, James could see the tension and fear clearly visible on their faces.

The loss of the patriarch would have been an impossible weight to bear at the best of times. But now, it was suffocating.

This family had suffered for so long. This was the third continent on which this ancient family feud had played out for them. All before they had truly re-connected as siblings and children. And the pressure was draining for all of them, not least his wife and partner and this was destroying the youngest, as brave as they were.

After a brief council, the wolves confessed to feeling out of place and uncomfortable this side of the sound. They were keen to head back to their home territory, not least to protect their dens.

On the other hand, James was reluctant to return with them with the broken family. But as they had all been forced into the centre of this conflict, he sadly knew that persisting to the bitter end was inevitable and the price for an enchanted heritage.

"We will be safer together," said Holly, an attempt at reassurance, but hardly relishing confronting the werewytch again. "And besides, we need to keep the circle of protection together and must have all of the changeling charms united for that cause."

At the mention of the circle her voice trailed away but her mother barely registered anything as she kneeled by her father's body.

James smiled at her courage. She was right, of course, Their advantage was in unity. But right now, unity was being tried as never before.

Feeling the need to do anything to ease the pain, the sisters returned to the ramshackle cottage leaving the adults to talk. Their intention was to explore the dark wytch's sinister handiwork.

The girls studied her use of the pentangle closely. Then they poked around at the foul-smelling brew still bubbling in the cauldron, even though the fire had long gone out.

Alice was on her knees by the iron range.

"What are you doing? Thought you'd have had enough of that dirty old oven," said Lucy. But her curiosity was pricked when Alice held a jar up to the light.

"What is that and why are you counting?" she asked.

"They're babies, my responsibility," she said, "I'm counting to make sure that every last one is there."

They stopped off at the dilapidated outhouse on the way back to the boat, where Alice opened the jar and tilted it on its side.

"I would say that is dry, dusty and insect-infested enough to serve as a fine new home for the next generation".

There was something appealing about life being restored to this dark place of suffering. So the young fae changeling smiled a precious smile, whispered a few last words in honour of her grandfather then turned and ran after her sisters, heading, once more, for the beach.

B y the time they made it back to the mountain tribe encampment, it was almost, quite aptly, the infamous witching hour.

The journey back through the forest had been enlightening. The smaller denizens let them know that Henry had returned this way, accompanied by a chilling figure shrouded in hooded clothes.

According to an owl, none dared to approach them because the aura she gave off warned that she was not here with good in her heart.

With all creatures afeared, there would be slim pickings for dinner tonight.

A bat stopped by to tell Alice that he had been up at the mountain tribe camp, hunting for moths which gather there during the full moon. The tribe's people left in a hurry, as word had reached them of the arrival of the dark sorceress.

So, when they arrived at the camp, sure enough, it was empty. Apart from a small fire burning by the ancient totem pole.

When they got closer, however, they could see that Henry, in human form, was seated by the fire.

Overjoyed, before the adults could say anything, the girls all rushed forward to greet their brother. But as they got close to him, he looked up suddenly and the look he gave them screamed, "NO!"

With a flash of combustible-driven bright light, an area the size of a large tent lit up around the changelings, capturing them all as assuredly as a dark magic net.

They were all stunned by the brightness and frustrated by the invisible bars. The effect of the light drained all the colour from their faces. It also seemingly dimmed their special powers, giving them the appearance of skeletons leaping about at a bizarre Halloween gathering.

As they panicked, with a dry, raking, wicked laugh Mohbreen stepped out from behind the totem pole.

"Well, well, well, little piglets," she cackled. "All of your noses are in my trough. There is no going back to your goddess sow now."

Without any warning, Bear lifted and threw his trident in one fluid movement, his brother having already started his own attack run.

Bill dropped to one knee and was taking aim at the target with his rifle, bolt working to load a slug while James raised his staff with malign intent.

"THIS has gone on for too long now, you denizen of darkness, the time of your reckoning is upon you," shouted the warlock, uncharacteristically losing his cool and channelling a lifetime of repressed and simmering hate.

With a wave of her bony hands, the crone changed the path of the trident. It slammed into the totem pole with a solid thump. And as it did, Henry screamed in agony as if the spear had pierced his heart.

Hawk had launched himself through the air, weapon before him like the nose of a fighter plane or beak of a raptor. But again, she blasted him with an unseen force, sending him clattering into the wooden carving.

This blow now sent Henry sprawling to the floor, as if the Indian's body had struck him direct.

Bill was adjusting the sights on his gun, but having just witnessed what she had, Elouisa, of all people, rendered it red hot with a wave of her hand. Bill dropped it with a betrayed shout and then looked up at his friend, confusion writ large on his face.

James had to choke back the curse he had started hurling when he realised, as his wife had, that the crone was using their talents against them. His mind was racing, they had to think fast.

But it was Elouisa, working on a hunch, who found the one thing her mother could never have considered. Walking briskly forward, she reached into the Everbag and withdrew the first of the mini sculptures she discovered.

Without examining it, she threw it into the fire.

"Brought your own wood, plain one? Do you intend to capture and burn me at the stake, daughter?" cackled the sorceress supreme, her confidence getting the better of her, blinding her to what was happening.

But as the study carving burned, a section of the totem pole, the bear and salmon, lit up, in a familiar jade green.

"The Rubyrobe," shouted Holly. "It's coming back to life," then, emboldened by its glow, she tentatively stepped through the light cage and moved to her mother's side.

As she did this, Elouisa reached for another of the carvings and also threw this into the flames.

This time, the great raven turned green, its features almost as animated as the giant corvid now seated, watching the action from the giant redwood tree.

Soon Alice was walking across to join the others, her profile crackling with jade light magic that emanated from her ring.

A blood curdling scream erupted from the mouth of their nemesis, enraged by what she had failed to foresee.

But by the time her fury had died down enough for her to focus, all the children bar Henry were free.

Now her ire became elemental, as all around her a vortex, a mighty whirlwind was gathering pace, plucking up everything in its path. With the demise of the druid, it appeared that her powers had grown. She had become the apex necromancer.

Yet as she started to bend elements to her will and turn the storm toward her antagonists, she first felt it stop and then saw it change direction and head back toward its source.

James and Elouisa were now controlling the vortex together.

"You forget," cried James, his voice travelling on the wind, "in nature, our Druidic roots are more powerful than your dark

Wiccan ways."

Timing it with care, she suddenly withdrew her resistance and stepped back behind the totem pole, letting the wild wind scream by.

This action threw the adults to the floor.

Now, when they looked up, she had Henry by the throat. Her sharp ebony wand was in her hand and it bit into his temple.

"It is time for you all to succumb to my will, or the next decision you make will be this foundling's last before I come for each and every one of you."

She pulled Henry across in front of the totem, not realising that they were now bathed in its green glowing light.

"You must have worked out by now, surely, that this is no man child?"

Her eyes lit up with dark glee as she spat out that phrase.

"No. Yours he is not, daughter. He was laid like a cuckoo egg in your forest nest."

Again, she was distracted and blinded by her own hatred and arrogance. She failed to notice that, once more, the top of the totem pole was starting to gather light.

"He is the product of the illicit coupling of the one you call the Prince of the Forest.

"He is the love that dare not speak its name.

He is Goddess Teote's eternal shame, conceived at full moon.

He is the child that should not have been.

He must be returned to darkness and must not be once again.

He must be sacrificed.

216

He must be returned to the spirit of the mountain."

As she screeched that last sentence, Henry's image on the totem filled with the last of the light.

Then Elouisa beckoned silently to Lucy, urging her daughter to deliver the killing stroke. In response to her mother's whispered advice, she instinctively felt in her pocket and found the black marble, the wolf's eye. Pausing to feel its cold reassurance fill her palm, she first raised it until she heard the wytch scream, then the youngest Savage cast this too into the blazing embers of the fire.

Suddenly, what was a green glow burned bright orange from the pinnacle carving's face.

As the wytch clutched the boy, she suddenly became conscious that the sinews in his neck were now bulging beneath her old fingers. Gradually soft skin gave way to fur. Now instead of bullying a small lad, she had a terrifying, snarling werebeast in her crooked hands. But more than that, this changeling had his changeling family around him, covering his back.

The wytch was eventually forced to release her grip, as now Henry rose to his feet, shaking her off like a limp blanket.

He then turned and took the crone's wrinkled and stone-cold hands in his, manually preventing the casting of any more spells.

She started to mutter an incantation. But to her horror, halfway through she found that her enfeebled mind could not recall the right words.

Then, looking up she noticed that the jade light tinged with orange from the totem had spread like lava. It now bathed the entire clearing where the forest creatures had started to gather.

Beams of elemental power radiated from the magical artefacts of each of the family and friends. They formed a semi-circular fan of energy, that was arching off and connecting with the totem, the focal point, the lightning rod.

But it was much more than just a totem now, it had become a gateway.

Finally, this portal to the ends of the earth was re-opening in its entirety, and something of extraordinary power was making its steady, relentless, inevitable way through.

Mohbreen screamed her contempt into the face of the changeling that held her fast, and the power of that raw hatred momentarily knocked him back.

She remained bathed in the magestream, the combined force of the family that was lost, now found. So she could neither fight nor flee.

But she had one last card to play.

Her greed for power.

The wytch looked up to the gathering dark shapes of the corvids in the trees.

"Nubia. This is your moment, ancient priestess of birds. Now is your chance to become my leader of the underworld beneath the mountain. Remember our pact, our promise? Now is the time. Summon your minions to my side."

The crow tilted its head to the side, as if thinking, then the other, fixing her in its black-beaded gaze.

The crow then spoke with the usual croaking caw, "But what use is a kingdom beneath a poison mountain, where nothing grows to feed the tasty creatures from which we in turn feed? Your dark magic brings little but misery, a kingdom of eternal night and destruction in which everything shrivels as old bones and nothing lush thrives. Without balance, nothing works. Nothing grows. All is dust and dry."

The words were like daggers.

The truth impossible to take.

And now, from the shadows, the wolves, ancient tribes, cougars, bears, including a certain cub and her mother and a host of animals of the forest floor moved closer in silence. While up above, every roost was being taken by the winged denizens of all shapes and sizes, both of the night as well as the day.

"So!" the werewytch screamed as if relieved. "I knew you would come. You are here to see the final crowning of your queen, are you not?"

She raised her arms for effect, but without her dark powers, this merely exaggerated her brittleness, her age her powerlessness. But pitifully, she bluffed on.

"You have come to pay your respects as one, to collect on my promises, having all done me some form of service along this path to destiny?"

But they were now looking past her, beyond her. They were looking to the path to the ancient mountain, whale-backed and once smoking, now lit up by the totem's light.

For there, silhouetted against the full blue moon, emerged the spirit deity, Hernunnos and his heart-matched lover for life, the earth goddess, Teote.

They had finally come at this joining of elements.

They were returning to restore much-needed balance.

They were crossing the veil to repair the wronged earth; to counter the poison in the Firehills.

They did not travel for retribution and vengeance.

They were here for forgiveness.

They were here to ensure justice.

They were here for atonement, to make amends.

They were here to end the pandemic of hate.

They appeared together to start the great age of peace.

But they required one last, overdue sacrifice to heal the toxic world.

They were here to collect on destiny's promise.

They had finally come, for her.

About the Author

English author Ian P Buckingham is widely published across a range of genres and mediums. A bit of a modern renaissance man, his work spans high-brow business books on brand and communication as well as magical adventure stories for children and young adults.

Winner of various creative writing prizes throughout his career and education in Africa and England, he has studied at Harvard as well as the University of Leeds where he also specialised in children's and Commonwealth literature.

Ian has edited several publications including poetry and creative writing magazines and has written, produced and directed plays. A proud father of two daughters (the muses for the important work) and a passionate shared parenting advocate, when not writing or roaming Britain's coastline and forests, Ian is a prominent management consultant and MBA lecturer, championing the crucial role of great stories in life generally, no matter the age of the reader.

Other books by Ian P Buckingham:

The Changeling Saga Book One: Legend of the Lost
The Changeling Saga Book Two: Ends of the Earth

For details of our other books, or to submit your own
manuscript please visit
www.green-cat.shop

Green Cat Books

Printed in Great Britain
by Amazon

71832723R00137